"What *were* your ambitions before you inherited the title, my lord?"

After hearing Lord Ashton's tragic story, Lily was curious and prompted him in a cautious compassionate voice.

Julian gave a bark of amused laughter. "Ha! You will be astonished! I was destined for the Church, Miss Clarke. *I* was to be the vicar of Pleasely!"

But Miss Clarke did not display astonishment, nor did she laugh. "On the contrary, I am not astonished. Rather I think I understand you better. To be *so* disillusioned as you are now, you must have been at some time as full of hope as I."

"Worse than you," Julian admitted. "Too hopeful, too trusting, too well-intended."

"You would have been a wonderful vicar," she said at last, her eyes narrowing speculatively. "I can just see you in your surplice... Quite handsome." Then, embarrassed, she looked away.

Julian laughed at her spontaneous candour but shook his head sadly.

" 'Tis all behind me now, Miss Clarke. Never to be."

Lily leaned forward to engage his complete attention. "It is *never* too late, my lord. For anything."

Books by Emily Dalton

HARLEQUIN REGENCY ROMANCE
31–A COUNTRY CHIT
44–AN INFAMOUS SEA BATH
59–BEAUTY AND THE BEASTIE
68–A HEAVENLY HOUSEGUEST

LILY AND THE LION

EMILY DALTON

Harlequin Books

TORONTO • NEW YORK • LONDON
AMSTERDAM • PARIS • SYDNEY • HAMBURG
STOCKHOLM • ATHENS • TOKYO • MILAN
MADRID • WARSAW • BUDAPEST • AUCKLAND

To Marmie,
It's life-confirming to know someone who believes in, and so deeply cherishes, the inherent goodness in all "God's Creatures." Thanks for being such a joy to write for and such a pleasure to know.

Published November 1992

ISBN 0-373-31185-0

LILY AND THE LION

CHAPTER ONE

JULIAN WINSLOW, Lord Ashton, looked down upon St. James's Street from the bow window at Whites. It was a damp, drear night, the street lamp on the corner casting a weak smudge of light into the thick fog. Having been shaded all day by a low balcony, the length of walkway opposite the exalted men's club was coated with a dingy slick of ice, making it necessary for passers-by to navigate their way with excruciating care.

Most of the people traversing the icy stretch were encumbered with packages and looked highly irritated by the inconvenience of either walking very slowly or falling down and losing everything they'd been struggling to hold on to—which included their dignity. Julian frequently could hear them cursing.

Ah, well. London in December was not especially conducive to lifting one's spirit, Julian concluded philosophically, trying to excuse his own stubborn melancholy, which hung on despite the many weeks that had passed since news of his nephew's death. He *himself* would certainly not be in London at such a damnable time of year if he hadn't wished to help his sister while she attended to business with her solicitor—business necessitated by Peter's death and the resulting upheaval of estate matters.

The dismal scene outside changed a little. A young man and woman were actually laughing as they slipped and slid about on the cobbles. They were attempting to step into a hired hack without falling down. The attempt proved to be futile, the both of them landing on their rumps.

The couple's outburst of merriment at finding themselves in such an embarrassing predicament, and the way they clung to each other, must have caused the hack driver to think the pair to be deep in their cups, because the frowning fellow flicked his dapple grey's ear with a crack of his whip and drove on. But Julian could see that the couple weren't inebriated, rather it was a case of April and May. They were in love. Julian's upper lip curled slightly and he turned away.

Fixing his jaundiced gaze on the gold tassels and fringe of the burgundy drapes pulled back from the tall windows, Julian contemplated the evening before him. A game of whist, a few tosses of hazard, perhaps. And maybe later he'd visit Monique. He'd not paid her a call for several days and he'd no doubt she'd be all in a pucker by now. French mistresses were famous for pouting when neglected and Monique played her part to the hilt.

Julian's gaze drifted back to the window and the view of the couple sprawled on the flagged walkway. He was helping her up now, shaking her skirt free of the grainy bits of frost that clung to it. She was straightening her fur-trimmed bonnet, smiling at her companion in the most intimate way....

CROSBY, THE HEAD BUTLER at Whites, had been standing at a respectful but noticeable distance from Lord Ashton for some time. He'd cleared his throat twice, yet his lordship still had not glanced his way. The elegant viscount appeared to be deeply engrossed in some scene outside the window, and a wistful smile played about his lips. Crosby cleared his throat again and waited, his thoughts going back to five years earlier, when Lord Ashton had first appeared on the London scene. Next to Brummel and Prinny, Julian Winslow was probably the most recognized figure in Town.

There were a plethora of young men with titles of equal or greater antiquity and with larger fortunes, though his lordship's fortune was certainly worth a plum. But despite the fact that he'd rusticated in Hampshire till the advanced age of five-and-twenty, when Lord Ashton did choose to show his face in Society, the ton liked what they saw. He quickly became the most sought-after guest for every hostess who had pretension to social glory. If his golden, sun-streaked thatch of hair was glimpsed towering above the milling crowd at any given function, said function was immediately pronounced a smashing success.

Lord Ashton's good looks could probably account for some of this popularity, but there was much more about him that inspired people's interest. The fact was, his looks were unique—not at all in the common way—and his personality matched his appearance. His prodigious height, his exotic golden eyes, his eccentric, Samson-like refusal to shear his waving blond hair short of his collar, his splendid figure and impeccable taste in clothing, his graceful, athletic stride and his aloof, wary demeanor and fang-sharp wit had earned him the ton's awed admiration and the epithet "The Lion."

He had also an interesting past. Everyone knew that the viscount's succession to his father's title was through tragedy, that tragedy being the death of his two elder brothers—one a victim of murder, the other of war. And everyone knew that his lordship had, as the youngest son, been destined for the clergy, and had even been most unfashionably enthusiastic at the notion of becoming a vicar. He'd not have hired a snivelling curate for stipend a month to oversee his parish, but would have personally watched over his flock with a benevolent eye.

Such enthusiasm for such a profession kept Julian in Hampshire and away from the frivolities of London for some time. But at the death of his beloved brothers and after a period of mourning, he'd emerged from the countryside a changed man. He was as cynical and jaded as the next fellow—nay, he was worse! Embracing the vices of Town life with a vengeance, he'd sinned with such efficient regularity that Old Harry himself would have been proud.

However, it was said that his lordship was an honest, honourable man who did not hurt or take advantage of anyone. He only indulged his excesses and debauchery in the company of men and women who were as jaded as he. He was also said to be a devoted brother to his one remaining sibling, a widowed sister. It was rumoured that he'd taken quite badly the news of his nephew's death at Waterloo several months ago. But it was difficult to imagine the aloof viscount caring very much about anything.

However, watching his lordship now, Crosby could have sworn he perceived a tender longing in that celebrated cynical expression. For a moment, he saw Lord Ashton as the vicar he might have been, wearing his surplice on Sabbath day.

"Crosby! What is it?"

Ah, he'd finally been noticed, but by the gruff tone of his lordship's voice, his presence wasn't appreciated. Crosby straightened and attached his gaze to a point just left of Lord Ashton's ear. "There's a note for you, my lord, just come from Albemarle Street." Crosby stepped closer and extended the silver salver on which reposed a small sheet of folded parchment paper.

Lord Ashton's brows lowered as he took the paper and read the message written there. Crosby waited at a discreet distance lest his lordship might need him to fetch quill and ink-horn for a reply. But Lord Ashton's concentration remained fixed on the paper for several moments beyond which might be expected in order to read the short missive.

"My lord?" Crosby ventured. "Do you wish me to fetch you some writing materials? Is there anything I can do?"

Lord Ashton's gaze swept about the room in a distracted fashion, as if seeking to settle upon something pleasing and finding that it was an impossible task. Crosby caught his eye for a second and was stirred by the stricken expression he perceived there.

"No, there's nothing you can do, Crosby," was his level, emotionless reply. "Except perhaps fetch my coat and hat, if you please. I'll be leaving." Lord Ashton then turned his back to the butler and propped his shoulder against the window embrasure, once more staring out at the drear December night.

"HE'S ALIVE, JULIAN! Peter's *alive!*"

Julian observed his elder sister with alarm and compassion. Her large blue eyes were brimmed with happy tears and her fading blond hair, grown so much greyer in the past few months, escaped her plain black cap in several places. When she'd summoned him from his club to her rented lodgings at Albemarle Street with a barely decipherable note claiming that she'd had a letter from Peter, Julian was filled with dread. And just as he'd feared, it seemed as though his grieving sister's fragile hold on reality had kicked over the traces at last. Apparently losing her husband and her only child within two years of each other was too much to bear.

"Winifred...Winny," he said soothingly, lifting his hands to grasp her thin shoulders. "You must know that's not true. Peter's gone. He was seen falling in battle. He died bravely, Winny, and you have every reason to be proud of your son. Had his father lived, Edward would have been proud, too. I know you loved Peter dearly, as did I, but you must accept—"

"You don't understand, Julian," Winifred interrupted, shrugging out of his gentle hold and beaming up at him with a smile that could light the cold, black night without. "It's true what I said in my note to you! I've a letter from him! He wrote to me! Come, I'll show you!"

Julian followed his sister from the entrance hall to the small parlour, his heavy black greatcoat and hat still in place. He held hope firmly in check as Winifred hurried to a satinwood table by the sofa, snatched up a sheet of thin writing paper and waved it in front of his longish and decidedly aristocratic nose. "Read it, dearest! It *is* from Peter. You know his handwriting. He's convalescing in a vicarage in a small town called Whitfield. He's been ill. He was unable to write till—"

Julian took the letter and examined the writing. Hope shook loose from his firm control and blossomed like the vibrant petals of spring's first flower. The writing was shaky, as if penned by a weak hand, but it *was* Peter's style! He thrust the letter back to his sister, saying in a voice brusque with emotion, "Hold this for me for just a moment while I take off my hat and coat, if you please! My temperature's shot up considerably since I entered this room."

Giggling like a schoolgirl, Winifred helped Julian out of his greatcoat and shallow-crowned beaver and tossed them to the butler. Flimwell caught the flying articles of clothing with considerable aplomb, and judging by the smile wreathing his usually grave and formal countenance, he didn't mind his mistress's lack of decorum in the least.

"Now, I'm going to sit down and go about this business in a calm manner," Julian stated carefully, inhaling a deep breath and easing his lanky frame down onto the sofa. His black jacket, breeches and waistcoat stood out starkly against the pale peach brocade of the couch, and also brought his shimmering aureate eyes into striking contrast. "I don't think I believe any of this, Winny. I dare not believe it." He dragged a slightly tremulous hand through his hair.

"You shall believe it all in a moment, little brother," Winifred assured him as she gleefully handed him the letter. Then she plopped down beside him and twined her small hands about his arm. "Read it aloud, Julian. I never tire of hearing those dear words! I've read it twice to the servants already, and thrice to Flimwell!"

Julian cleared his throat and began.

"Dear Mama,

I daresay you'll be deuced surprised to hear from me, as I suspect you were informed of my death some weeks ago! I'm dreadfully sorry if you've suffered, Mama, but I'm very much alive and itching to come home in time for Christmas! I'm staying in the vicarage at Whitfield, a town just north of Dover. I've been abed here for some time, but—don't worry!—I haven't any permanent injuries. I did sustain a bullet wound at Waterloo, and in the confusion directly after the war, I was unable to get word to you of my safety. I reached Dover in quite good health, but was set upon by a footpad that first night while I was awaiting some means of transportation home. I confess, Mama, I was in my altitudes and not exactly in prime twig for fending off a thief. He knocked me out and stole all my money and clothes. I was unconscious off and on for several weeks before I recovered sufficiently to tell the good Vicar Clarke who I am and to write you a letter. The vicar and his family have treated me like royalty and have looked after my every need. I'm especially grateful to their eldest daughter, Lily—a darling girl! Such a vision I woke up to with her sweet face poised above me! I thought I'd died and gone to Heaven! But I digress. Tell Julian to come and fetch me! I'm still weak and needs must bring a nurse along on the journey. My directions are..."

"Et cetera, et cetera." Julian leaned back and drew Winifred against him in a fierce hug. "The rascal!" he growled. "Even if the handwriting had been unrecognizable, there's no mistaking that this is a letter from Peter. No one but my maggoty nephew awakes from a concussed brain and falls immediately in love!"

"Don't you dare call him names, Julian!" Winifred chided playfully. "I've plans to spoil him shamefully when he arrives home!"

Julian raised a tawny brow. "As if he isn't already spoiled beyond redemption! Do you suppose this Lily Clarke is the nurse he means to bring along on the journey? I hope he won't be too disappointed when her parents quite wisely refuse to allow her to accompany two bachelors on a protracted journey requiring at least one night at an inn! I wonder if it was the vicar who found Peter, or if someone else found him and took him to the vicarage? And where was he shot? In the arm, or perhaps a leg? He doesn't give many details."

"I'm just thankful he's alive and tolerably well, if we may believe his report," Winifred said, a small frown puckering her forehead. Then her brow cleared and she smiled archly. "Mayhap he's truly fallen in love with this Lily. I had hoped he would choose one of the Cavendish twins, but I shall be happy with whomever he finally chooses if it means I can become a grandmother at last!"

"I shouldn't count on a match just yet, Win. A passing fancy, I suspect," Julian cautioned her.

"Just because you've never fallen in love doesn't mean Peter can't," Winifred retorted as she pushed herself up from the sofa and turned to face her brother.

"Don't be naïve, Winny. Peter's in a vulnerable position just now. And upon reflection, he'll probably realize that Miss Clarke would not be a suitable wife. They move in very different circles, you know."

Winny crossed her arms and looked at him consideringly. "You aren't dismissing her as eligible simply because she's a vicar's daughter, are you? They might come of quite good family and enjoy a comfortable living at Whitfield."

"It's not a matter of genealogy or funds, Winifred," her brother scoffed, waving an elegant hand. "It's just—"

"It's just your personal prejudice against the clergy," Winifred asserted quietly, "and this from a man who once intended to make the Church his livelihood."

Julian's gaze shifted and his eyes clouded with unwelcome memory. "But that was before I inherited the title. Before Tom and Richard were killed."

"But I'll wager you'd still rather be a vicar than a viscount," Winifred persisted.

Julian's expression grew cold as he gave his jacket sleeve a tug. "Why would any sane man wish for such a thing? However, if it could bring back our brothers, I'd happily take my vows! But it won't. Nothing will. And things being as they are, I've no desire to embrace a profession that beguiles gullible people into believing that the world is a benevolent place."

"Oh, Julian, you're hopeless!" said Winifred, throwing up her arms in exasperation. "You've become the most dreadful cynic! You must admit that Providence has been merciful in returning to us our dear Peter!"

"Yes, in this instance we were lucky," Julian agreed with a dismissive shrug of his shoulders. Then he added, with a hint of a smile, "I suggest that you count your blessings and do not hang your happiness on the slim chance of snagging a daughter-in-law!"

"Oh, I shan't, Julian. I'm too happy and too blessed to dare hope for anything more than Peter's safe return! And I am eternally indebted to the Clarkes for taking such good care of him. After all these weeks of imagining him in some shallow grave on foreign soil, I can hardly believe..." Winifred pressed a hand against her mouth, tears springing to her eyes as emotion overcame her.

Julian stood and draped a long arm about his sister's shoulders. "You will certainly believe it when I pull up in front of Ashton House with Peter in tow. I want you to spend Christmas there, Winny. Besides, Peter's estate in Derbyshire is so much greater a distance, he would be fagged to death by the time he got there. After the holidays, he should be rested sufficiently to resume his journey. Oh, and you had best advise your solicitor that Edward's nephew, Reginald, must be informed that his inheritance has been stymied by Peter's miraculous return from the grave! What else should we discuss before I go? You will begin packing immediately, I suppose?''

"But I want to go with you, Julian! I want to see Peter as soon as possible," Winifred protested, pulling away to turn pleading eyes to Julian.

"You know I can travel much more expeditiously alone, my dear. And it is wretchedly damp and cold. Peter would not wish you to become ill. I suspect your health is a little frail just now. Your time would be best spent supervising the decoration of Ashton, eating Cook's most nourishing dishes and sleeping every day till noon. Let Peter come home to a cheerfully bedecked house and a plump, rosy mother!''

Winifred propped her hands on her small hips and shook her head, a wide, resigned smile lighting her face. Julian's heart swelled with gratefulness for the return of that girlish smile. "You'd persuade the very devil to do your bidding, Julian Winslow! I'll stay at Ashton, and I'll decorate every chamber in that grand old house till every holly bush in Hampshire is pruned nearly to the roots. But you'd better have my son home for Christmas, or I'll have your handsome hide to hang in Edward's trophy chamber! You have a little less than a fortnight to accomplish it, you know!''

Julian threw back his head and laughed heartily, the deep basso tones echoing down the hall and into the kitchen, where the scullery maids exchanged sighs and smiles. Julian's laugh was as rare as a snow flurry in August, and it had been a long time since the servants at No. 12 Albemarle Street had had the delight of hearing "The Lion's" roar.

"Oh, Winny. How I've longed to hear you threaten and scold me, just as you used to do. Will you never see me as more than your little brother?" he teased.

Winifred's eyes softened. "If I did not think you the most capable, caring man ever born, next to my dear Edward—God rest his soul!—I would not entrust to you my invalid son."

"Your perception of me is singular, Winny," Julian said caustically, showing a sudden change of mood. "You're blinded by our sibling bond, I suppose. I'm not known hereabouts as a particularly 'good' man. Most people think me a cold, uncaring devil." He paused. "And by my own estimation, I do believe they're right."

"They don't know you as I do, Julian," Winifred informed him sternly. "And you don't know yourself, either, for that matter!" she added, poking his waistcoat buttons with a small finger. "Inside that lion's chest beats the heart of a—"

"Lord, don't say it!" Julian protested with a goodnatured grimace. "What an unmanly thought to possess the heart of a lamb, or an angel, or some such sentimental claptrap!" Then, before she could say more, Julian bent down and kissed his sister on the forehead. "I'll leave first thing in the morning. Where's my coat? I've much to do! Ah, thank you, Flimwell!"

Flimwell, who had been watching from the door the entire time, rushed forward with Julian's greatcoat and hat and assisted the gentleman into them. With one last hug and kiss for Winny, Julian strode to the door with a jungle cat's easy, muscled grace. Flimwell opened the door and Julian passed through, touching the rim of his hat in a friendly gesture to the thin, middle-aged butler.

Julian descended the steps and traversed the short walkway to the gate of the wrought-iron fence surrounding the small front court of the angular Town house. He lifted his head to the leaden skies. Soot and fog commingled and hung over the city like a funeral shroud. Or so it had seemed to him on his way to Winifred's. Now he imagined the thick grey air as a downy wool blanket, seeming to buffet the buildings against the cold.

Julian's footsteps echoed in the empty neighbourhood, while in the distance a watchman chanted the time in a resonant monotone. Most of the windows of the elegant Town houses were shuttered and the knockers removed from the front doors. The ton were in the country for the holidays, leaving the more fashionable areas of London all but deserted.

Out of the corner of his eye, Julian saw a flickering shadow across the flagged walkway. He turned, but perceived nothing out of the ordinary and no one skulking in the dark. However, he still reached inside his greatcoat pocket and curled his fingers round the comforting handle of the small pistol he carried with him at all times. He'd not be caught unawares like his too-trusting brother, Richard. No, not he.

After a time, Julian grew more relaxed and pulled his hand from out of his pocket to rub the tip of his cold nose. His extremities might be cold, but for the first time in a long time, his heart was heating his insides like a balmy summer sun. Peter was alive! And he had only to fetch him home to bring laughter and hope back into his sister's life.

Julian's brows furrowed. But what about this Lily Clarke? He fervently hoped that she would not prove to be a nuisance. A passing fancy, that's all it was that Peter was feeling for her, he was sure. She might very well be moralistic and parochial—certainly no match for Peter, who lived life with a dash of deviltry that would probably offend a prissy vicar's daughter. She'd only known him as an invalid—weak and compelled to stay abed. She wasn't really acquainted with the real Peter at all.

Ah well, as soon as he got Peter away from the Whitfield Vicarage, Julian was quite sure Miss Lily Clarke would be soon forgotten.

"DR. PAYNE, don't you dare use those slimy little beasts on Captain Wendover!" Lily remonstrated as the doctor leaned over Peter's bed. "He's never been leeched and, as you know yourself, he's done very well without resorting to such extremes."

White-haired, stout Dr. Payne straightened and eyed Lily sternly. "I know your opinion about leeches, Lily.

And though I've brought a jar with me today, I had not intended to use them on Captain Wendover. I merely set them on the table so that I might have better access to the other instruments in my bag. No need to fly into a miff, m'dear! I've kept the fellow alive this long, haven't I?''

Lily tucked a stray wisp of glossy chestnut hair behind her ear and smiled with relief. "I beg your pardon, sir," she said repentantly, though her brown eyes twinkled merrily. "But when I saw the jar sitting upon the table, and with the morning sun glinting off the glass so brightly, making those, er... least comely of God's creatures look so *ghastly*, I could not prevent myself from offering comment!''

Dr. Payne lifted a large, rough hand and lightly pinched Lily's cheek. "You can always prevent yourself from speaking, Lily, and many a time would have done yourself a great service by keeping silent.''

"Lily can't help being outspoken," came a youthful voice from behind the doctor. "And she's always right, y'know! Knows more than any sawbones *I've* ever clapped eyes on!''

Dr. Payne turned back to the bed and scowled at the pale, fair-haired young man reclining against two plump feather pillows. Though Peter was all of five-and-twenty, in his present frail condition he looked much younger. "Excepting yourself, of course," Peter amended, his hazel eyes wide and ingenuous.

Lily dropped her gaze to the rag rug that covered the wood floor and stifled a giggle.

"I never said she didn't have a good head on her shoulders," grumbled Dr. Payne. "However, I *do* think her heart sometimes overrules—"

"A good head, indeed. A pretty head, too," Peter interrupted, in the admiring voice he sometimes used when he was behaving like a mooncalf. Lily's urge to laugh quickly dissipated. She did not like such a tone of voice in Peter. His obvious tendre for her disturbed her very much. She did not return his feelings and had always worried that his infatuation for her might interfere with her duties as nurse. Above all else, she wanted Peter to get well and be taken home to his grieving mother. Thank goodness Peter's uncle was expected to arrive today to do just that.

Dr. Payne cleared his throat, his keen eyes shifting back and forth between the two of them. "As I was saying—and I'm sure Lily won't take umbrage in my plain speaking, since I've known her since she was no taller than my boot top—her propensity to take personal interest in every unfortunate case that comes her way may someday prove to be...ill-advised! Such undiscriminating charity is in variance with the good sense I know she has!"

"I'm certainly glad she didn't look the other way and spare herself the trouble of nursing *me* back to health!" Peter exclaimed with feeling. "I shall be forever grateful that she saw me as I lay face down in the dirt!"

Frustrated with being persistently misunderstood, the good doctor sighed and said, "I'm not speaking of you, Captain Wendover, but these cats, for example…" He waved his arm in a sweeping gesture. There was a calico cat stretched out on the window-sill, its front paws tucked under its chest, its head raised to the sun in a sphinx-like pose, its eyes shut. There was a black kitten by the fireplace, batting around an old tassel from a discarded slipper. There was a grey tabby on the end of the bed, nestled against Peter's feet. "And the rest of the house is similarly decorated, I might add!" he finished.

"A cat at the end of the bed works as well as a hot brick," Lily defended, "and you know we only have six cats altogether, Dr. Payne. It's just that they like Peter and spend much of their time in here. Besides, I think cats can be a soothing influence in a sickroom. Shadrack, Jonas and Eve are comforting companions for Peter."

"They do very well when *you're* otherwise occupied, Lily," Peter said teasingly. "But you know I'd rather have your company than any other," he added in much too serious a tone to suit Lily.

"She's been a good nurse for you, Captain," the doctor said, putting away his instruments. "I understand you'll be leaving us as soon as your family sends transportation. But I don't want you thinking you can resume all your former activities willy-nilly. There will be a period of recovery that must be strictly adhered to, or there's a possibility that the fever may return."

"Lily shall see that I stay in bed," Peter replied, smiling in such a way that Lily felt the colour creeping up her face to the very roots of her hair. Again she contemplated the rag rug.

"Is Lily accompanying you on your journey, Captain?" asked the doctor, tidying up from his task, then removing his spectacles and making quite an absorbing business out of the cleaning of them against the front of his black frock-coat.

"I've asked her to, but she keeps me in suspense. But if she doesn't, I shall have to ask Janet to come in her stead."

Lily's head jerked up. "Peter, how can you be so shatterbrained! Janet doesn't have the slightest notion how to bring down a fever! Why, she can barely keep up with her duties as abigail!"

"Another charity case, that one," mumbled the doctor.

Peter shrugged his shoulders, the bedgown bagging about his thin shoulders—shoulders that had been thick with muscle when he'd first been brought to the vicarage in the back of the dray. Lily wanted to see those shoulders strong and firm and muscled again. "It's either you or Janet. Next to you, Janet's the prettiest girl in the house. No offence to your sister, Rachael, but *she's* only seven."

"Your logic is not sound, young man," said the doctor drily. He turned to Lily. "It would be a shame to lavish so much attention on a patient only to lose him at the last to Janet's ignorance. I know of two or three ladies in the neighbourhood who would be qualified and capable—"

Peter crossed his arms over his chest and lifted his chin. "If I can't have Lily as nurse, I won't have anybody," he said stubbornly, looking for all the world like a child instead of the grown man he was.

Dr. Payne frowned. "You're not being at all reasonable, Captain."

Lily heaved a large sigh. "And I expect he does not intend to become more reasonable as the time draws near for his departure. I suppose I had better go with him—with a chaperon for myself, of course. I'm sure my parents will not object. I've already discussed the possibility with them, and they were not opposed."

The doctor raised a brow and muttered something again, this time so low Lily barely heard him. "No, I suspect they weren't. Less worldly sense than a pair of babes!"

Wisely ignoring the doctor's comments, Lily wagged her finger in Peter's face. "But I'll not spend more than a day or two with you, Peter, once we've reached your uncle's estate in Hampshire, since you say he'll certainly take you there first. I'm sure I can instruct your manservant and your mother in the proper care to be taken of you and then leave without another thought for your safety."

"That you would leave me at all, and without another thought of me, pains me desperately, Lily," Peter bemoaned, screwing up his face into an expression of theatrical woe. "Surely you don't mean it?"

Lily opened her mouth to retort in her most quelling, no-nonsense, matronly voice, but was forestalled by the sudden appearance of Janet's mob-capped head poking in at the door. "La, miss! There's a fine carriage pulled up in front o' th' house. All shiny black and grey, with beautiful horses t'pull it! And another spankin' carriage behind it!" Then she flipped her long blond braid over her shoulder and went briskly down the hall, her peg-leg beating a tattoo on the wood floor.

Peter's hazel eyes deepened in colour and brightened in anticipation. "Uncle Julian!" he shouted, sitting up abruptly, so abruptly that he weaved to and fro from the violent movement.

Lily reached across the bed to steady him by grasping his arms. "Be still, Peter! I'm sure Mama will bring him up to you immediately."

"I want to go to the window," Peter objected. "I want to see if it's truly him!"

"You've been out of bed once already this morning and worn yourself quite out, Lily tells me," said the doctor, leaning down to place a restraining hand on Peter's shoulder.

"Then you go to the window, Lily!" Peter pleaded. "Tell me how the gentleman looks as he comes up the walk. Then I'll know if it's Julian!"

Lily readily obeyed. She was curious to see Peter's uncle, too. From all that Peter had told her, Lord Ashton ought to be quite worth looking at. She'd never seen Peter so agitated. The excitement in his manner was infectious and she hurried to the window to look out, ready to be awed by the stately appearance of "The Lion." Her hand flew to her mouth and her brown eyes widened.

"Well? Well? What do you see?" called Peter.

"Oh dear, what's to do?" said Lily, but with a definite hint of amusement behind the concerned words. "I see a very tall man with long yellow hair dampening his trousers by sitting in the snow, his hat upside down in Papa's thorny rose-bush, and with a most disgruntled expression on his face!"

Peter slapped his leg and gave a shout of laughter. "Good God, it *is* Uncle Julian!"

CHAPTER TWO

FROM THE VANTAGE POINT of his carriage window that crisp winter morning, Julian had thought the vicarage a remarkably peaceful-looking dwelling. The house was large and rambling, and the brick from which it was constructed had, over the years, weathered to a mellow, golden hue. The low stone wall enclosing the immediate grounds was picturesque, and though the vines that covered it were now leafless and layered with fresh-fallen snow, Julian could well imagine how charming would be the aspect in spring. Smoke curled from three different chimneys, suggesting a snug interior.

Quite delightful, he thought grimly. But who knew what manner of people resided inside? He would not allow himself to be unduly influenced by the pleasing exterior of the vicarage. Though he was grateful to the Clarkes for nursing Peter back to health, and therefore was predisposed to like them, he must be on his guard. They might be toadeaters hoping to advance themselves through their new acquaintance with Peter. Judging by the size of the house and by Whitfield itself, Vicar Clarke's living was probably quite comfortable, as long as he didn't have a quiver full of children to support. If they descended from reasonably good stock, Julian wouldn't be surprised to learn that they had encouraged Peter's infatuation for Lily and were hopeful of an alliance. Tired of speculation about the Clarkes and their motives, and most anxious to see Peter, Julian prepared to alight. Grown warm from the morning sun beating against the carriage roof, he first removed his greatcoat.

After he'd stepped down from the carriage and progressed a few feet past the gate, Julian knew his first impression of the vicarage as being peaceful to have been entirely misleading. With a sound like a stampede of swine, a thundering noise and high-pitched squeals could be heard approaching from behind the house. Then, before he'd time to assimilate the cause of the commotion and comprehend that he was about to be run over by a pack of sledding children, it was too late.

They came round the corner of the house at a speed impossible to abandon at short notice. How many of them there were was hard to tell. Julian managed to jump out of the way, but in so doing he lost his footing and landed on his backside in two inches of wet snow.

After a moment of shocked disbelief, as he felt the damp invade the seat of his pantaloons and the snow trickle down the tops of his Hessian boots (no doubt to puddle later in the toes and heels of his stockings), a small, freckled face presented itself not six inches from his nose. Large, almond-shaped brown eyes, thickly lashed, stared at him.

"Are you hurt, thir?"

Julian blinked and answered curtly, "No. Who the deuce are you? One of the little ruffians who tried to run me over, I suppose?"

The face, wrapped all about in a blue knitted scarf, solemnly swivelled from side to side. "Oh, no, thir," the child lisped. "I'm just their thithster, Rachael."

No further conversation was possible at this point, because Julian was suddenly overcome with people wishing to help him up. His coachman, his valet, the aforementioned ruffians (who had apparently repented of their discourtesy and were bent on making reparation) and a tall, gentlemanly looking man with grey flecked hair, whom Julian assumed must be the Vicar Clarke, descended upon him all at once and tried to grab his arms to give him a heave-ho.

Concerned that he might be killed by kindness, or at the very least relieved of an appendage, Julian tucked his elbows against his sides and levered himself up without any assistance at all. Cutting into the distressed babble of his servants, the jabbering of the children—there were five by quick count—and the vicar's murmured expressions of sincere concern, Julian said loudly, "I'm quite all right, just wet! Do go back to the carriage, Jem, and you, too, Pleshy! I shall need a change of clothes. Vicar Clarke, I presume?"

Julian spoke with as much calm dignity as he could muster, though he knew he sported a giant circle of wet on his backside. And it was none too comfortable, either, what with the breeze coming up from behind as it was.

"Yes, and you are Lord Ashton, Peter's uncle." Vicar Clarke smiled, sketched a quick bow and motioned towards the house. "We won't chit-chat here, my lord. Please come in and warm yourself by the fire till your manservant brings a change of clothing for you. And please accept my humble apologies for the children. They're an active lot and sometimes not as careful as they should be." The speech was delivered with good humour and graciousness, and did not indicate excessive deference or insincerity. Julian grudgingly allowed that, upon first encounter at least, the vicar was not a toadeater.

Julian bowed his acceptance of this apology and preceded the vicar to the house, not entirely sure whether or not he'd heard a wayward giggle escape from the gaggle of children that remained outside. Just as he was about to enter the house, Julian felt a tug at his coat-tails. He looked down and discovered Rachael proffering him his hat. It looked quite disreputable. There were thorn holes in the crown and snow melting on the rim.

"Thith ith yours, thir," Rachael told him solemnly.

"So it is," he replied equably, disarmed despite himself at the little girl's determination to be helpful. "I should recognize it anywhere. Thank you, Rachael!" He took the hat and carried it into the house.

Inside he was greeted by Mrs. Clarke, a petite woman with dark brown hair and small, serene features, dressed in a simple cambric round gown. After a brief "How do you do?" she bustled him over to stand in front of a roaring fire. While his valet, Pleshy, retrieved his portmanteau from the carriage boot, Julian was at leisure to observe his surroundings and the inhabitants of Whitfield Vicarage.

The parlour in which he presently toasted his derriere was small and the furnishings a little worn and shabby, like the dog-eared pages of a well-loved book. But the room was clean, though comfortably cluttered with several objects of employment or amusement. On the floor by a rocking chair was an open sewing box with a half-finished pair of rose pink slippers beside it. There was a game of chess set out on a table near the fire. An easel with a water-colour ocean scene propped upon it stood near the window. And there were three cats in the room—one on the mantelshelf, one on the sofa arm and the last twining itself round and between Julian's boots.

"Oh, dear," said Mrs. Clarke, observing the yellow-striped cat with mild interest. "I do believe Simon's taken a fancy to you, Lord Ashton. I hope you don't mind?"

Then, without waiting for his reply (perhaps assuming that he didn't mind in the least, or perhaps thinking he was positively mad for cats), Mrs. Clarke smiled and said, "I'll have Cathy bring you some tea.

You must be hungry, too. Sweet biscuits will be the very thing.''

"Really, Mrs. Clarke, that won't be necessary," Julian demurred, raising a hand in polite protest. "You can imagine that I'm most anxious to see my nephew. How is he?''

Vicar Clarke, who'd been helping Rachael out of her coat, her mittens, her boots, and the several yards of scarf wound about her head, came and stood beside Julian at the fireplace, while Rachael sat beside her mother on the sofa. Rachael and her mother looked very much alike. They were even dressed similarly.

"Peter is doing well," said the vicar, stretching his hands to the fire and turning them up, then down, then up again, just as though he were toasting bread. "But he was in very bad shape when we found him lying by the side of the road on the outskirts of town, and I don't think you should expect too much when first you see him.''

Julian felt a tremor of foreboding. "Peter indicated in his letter that he had not suffered any permanent injuries. May I believe his report?''

"You may, but he's still very weak. Thank goodness the blow to his head did not remove his memory. We were afraid at first that it had. He was terribly befuddled for so long. But then he slowly regained his senses and is now as lively and mentally alert as one could wish for. As I said, however, physically he's quite weak. He sleeps a great deal, but that is as it should be.''

Julian nodded, impressed with the vicar's calm, unadorned statement of facts. "I understand. Can you tell me where he received the bullet wound?''

"In the left shoulder. It's still a little stiff, but our Dr. Payne assures us that in time he will regain all of his former strength and movement in that joint.'' The vicar smiled reassuringly. "Time. That's the ticket, Lord Ashton.''

While Julian pondered the irony of a physician named "Dr. Pain,'' a quick step was heard in the hall and he glanced towards the door in hopes of seeing his valet. While his backside was nearly dry, water squished between his toes most uncomfortably. But instead of Pleshy, in strode a young woman in a yellow dress as simply tailored as her mother's.

Yes, there could be no mistaking that this young woman was daughter and sister to the two other females in the room. She had the same shiny, chestnut-coloured hair and the same almond-shaped dark eyes fringed with thick lashes. Her figure was trim and pleasing. Her carriage was feminine and light, but, in Julian's opinion, a trifle too "bouncy,'' as if she were bursting with that most unfashionable sentiment called enthusiasm. Horrors! Julian had a constitutional distrust of undiscriminating cheerfulness! Was this "bouncy'' young woman the infamous Lily who'd beguiled Peter's susceptible heart? She *was* pretty, but certainly not out of the common way.

"Goodness, Papa!" she exclaimed before she'd taken more than three steps into the room. "How do you dare keep Lord Ashton downstairs when you know Peter is positively *wild* to see him?" She stood in front of her father, but turned her wide, curious gaze to Julian and smiled. "And I would wager that Lord Ashton is just as anxious to see Peter!"

"Peter knows that his uncle is here, then?" queried Mrs. Clarke from the sofa as she composedly brushed and arranged Rachael's snow-dampened hair into a neat plait. "But he must wait, because Lord Ashton fell victim to your unruly brothers and needs must change his clothes."

"I know," revealed the young lady, with a definite twinkle in her expressive eyes and a suppressed grin lurking at the corners of her mouth. She tucked a stray strand of smooth hair behind her ear. "I saw the rumpus from the upstairs window. A dreadfully shabby way for my ramshackle brothers to welcome a guest to the house, I must admit. But a little dampness does not signify, does it, my lord? Cannot you change your clothes later? Peter is beside himself with impatience to see you!"

"Lord Ashton, this is my eldest child, Lilith," said the vicar, gazing fondly at his daughter, and seemingly unmoved by her forwardness in speaking so frankly to a gentleman to whom she had as yet not even been introduced. But, Julian admitted to himself, her forwardness did not strike him as being of the flirtatious variety, like the archness sometimes assumed by the brassy little coquettes who were invariably part of the London Marriage Mart. Miss Lilith Clarke just seemed to be uncommonly friendly and outspoken. Horrors! he again thought. Such excess of amiability could be quite fatiguing.

"If anyone would understand my wish to be comfortable, Miss Clarke," said Julian, with a slightly mocking edge to his voice, "it would be Peter. Before he was a soldier, he was a rather spoiled tulip of the ton. Comfort was a priority with Peter, and probably still is. I understand you have stood as nurse to him. I hope he's not been too demanding?"

Miss Clarke raised her brows, as if surprised and a little disbelieving. "Indeed, I'm amazed to learn that Peter has ever been spoiled. He's been an exceptional patient." Now her brows drew together and she added musingly, "No doubt his experiences in the army have cured him of that sort of selfishness, for I perceive no overconcern with his own comfort now. Peter has withstood a great deal of pain and discomfort for several weeks with scarcely a complaint."

Julian observed to himself that Peter must have been acting the Trojan to gain Miss Clarke's approval. Never mind, it probably had done the fellow good. But now it would seem completely frivolous and selfish if *he* were to insist on changing his clothes before visiting Peter. Truth to tell, he really was extremely anxious to see his nephew and could, indeed, tolerate a little dampness for a while.

"Will you take me to his room, Miss Clarke?" Julian asked her.

"Certainly I shall," she replied, smiling happily. "You're the best medicine Peter could possibly have today! Are you ready, then?"

"Ready and willing," he said amiably, but with a wry undertone. Miss Clarke seemed to catch the nuance of mockery in his voice and she flashed him a searching look. So, Miss Clarke was no thimblewit. That was a surprise, because it had been his opinion that most determinedly cheerful people were prone to be silly and addle-pated. How interesting that she appeared to be neither.

Pulling his gaze reluctantly away from Miss Clarke's intelligent brown eyes, he turned to Vicar Clarke, and without a trace of his former mockery, feelingly thanked him. "I am deeply indebted to you and your good wife for saving my nephew's life. My sister sends her warmest thanks, too. Indeed, I believe she is planning to pen you a letter expressing those sentiments. She and I are both painfully aware that if you hadn't come along that night and found him, then took him in—"

The vicar smiled and waved his hand dismissively. "We did nothing beyond what any good Christian would do. And we've all grown very fond of Peter. He's a brave lad."

Julian wondered if Miss Clarke was even fonder of Peter than were her parents. He hoped not, because despite his growing good opinion of the Clarke fam-

ily, Julian still believed that Lily's provincial upbringing would make her an unsuitable wife for Peter, who
was very much a man of the Town. He pondered these
thoughts as he followed Miss Clarke into the hallway.
There he saw his valet finally coming through the door
with his portmanteau. Pleshy, half-French, half-Scots,
cut rather a dash amongst the servant set with his thick
black hair and engaging manners.

"Just a tad late, Pleshy," he murmured placidly as
he followed Miss Clarke up the stairs. The yellow-
striped cat came fast and silently on his lordship's
heels. Behind him, Julian could hear his valet indulging a violent fit of sneezing. Ah, yes, now he remembered. Pleshy was physically intolerant to cats.

HOLDING UP HER SKIRTS with both hands as she as-
cended the stairs to the upper floor, Lily glanced over
her shoulder at Lord Ashton. He was studying the
landscapes hanging on the wall, or at least appeared
to be. Lily wondered if such a proud-looking, elegant
gentleman was capable of feeling the apprehension
that would be natural under the circumstances. She
wondered if he were frightened of what he might see
when he entered Peter's room.

When she'd first seen the viscount in an upright
position, standing in front of the fire, she'd thought
he was quite the tallest, most imposing personage
she'd ever encountered in the entire course of her one-
and-twenty years. It was no mystery to her why the ton
had attached to this nobleman the glorious epithet of

"The Lion." But, goodness, she had not expected him to so vividly live up to Peter's proud description of him!

They were at the top of the stairs now and she motioned that he should follow her down the hall. She smiled at him, but he seemed preoccupied, aloof. The passage was wide and they walked abreast, so she took the opportunity to dart a glance or two at him before they reached Peter's room at the end of the hall. The burgundy jacket he wore encased his broad shoulders precisely. An ivory brocade waistcoat and meticulously tied, blindingly white neckcloth brought out the winter-whipped hue in his high cheekbones. And the buff-coloured pantaloons and well-polished boots clung to the lean, muscled lines of his legs to such an exactness ... Well, Lily quite blushed at her own brazen appreciation of a man's attractions!

From a high forehead his wheat-coloured hair fell in full, graceful waves down to his collar in the back. His brows were arched and at least two shades darker than his hair. His nose was straight and slightly long, his lips firm and narrow, his chin and jawline strong, hinting of stubbornness. His eyes ...

She opened the door to Peter's bedchamber. Lord Ashton's eyes—those odd, golden eyes—had been cool, reserved, assessing as he walked the length of the hall. Now as he regarded Peter, these same eyes lit and darkened to sparkling amber. The firm lips parted over straight white teeth. To see his lordship's striking features so animated made Lily's heart actually flutter! Emotion transformed him from a well-sculpted but stone-cold statue to a devastatingly handsome, warm human being.

STANDING AT THE DOOR, Julian looked about the small bedchamber with a mixture of curiosity and intense anticipation. The furniture was heavy and old-fashioned, bathed in the sunshine that streamed between the open draperies of two forward-facing windows. A calico cat reposed on the window-sill, and the yellow-striped tom that had followed Julian from the parlour joined a black kitten at play on a sunny patch of wood floor by the armoire.

A stout, bespectacled gentleman stood by the bed. But with the exception of a grey cat stretched out at the foot of it, the bed was empty. Julian's anxious gaze darted about the room till it lighted on Peter, sitting in a rocking chair drawn comfortably close to a brisk fire. He was facing away from the door and did not immediately perceive that Julian had entered the room.

Even from an angle, Julian could tell that his nephew was a haggard shadow of his former self. But when Peter turned and saw him standing there, his voice rang out with all the youthful verve Julian remembered. "Julian! You've come!"

Joy and pain struggled together for the upper hand—joy to see Peter, pain to see him so wasted, so pale. Julian moved forward, towards the thin figure tucked all round with a heavy brown coverlet. He forced a smile to his lips, then felt it become more genuine the closer he got to his nephew.

When he reached the chair, Julian drew Peter into a smothering embrace, tempering his strength when he felt the frail frame of his nephew tremble beneath his large hands. "God, Peter, we thought you were... I can't tell you how much... Your mother..."

"Julian, it's so good to see... If you only knew how I've longed... Mother, how is...?"

Somehow it didn't seem important that neither of them could finish a sentence. They were communicating quite well, anyway. Despite his misgivings about Peter's appearance, and despite his poor opinion of forced or arbitrary cheerfulness, when Julian at last drew back, he determined to look as cheerful as possible.

"So, my good fellow, are you ready to come home with me? Your mother awaits us at Ashton House and has promised to skin me if I don't deliver you to her by Christmas!" He shifted his gaze to the bespectacled fellow in the rumpled frock-coat, whom he assumed was the doctor, partly because he wished to speak with him and partly because he needed time to compose himself. It would never do to show such strong emotion to Peter. Julian itched to get him home to Ashton where he could fatten him up with Cook's most tempting cuisine.

Julian stepped forward and extended his hand. "How do you do? I'm Lord Ashton. You must be the physician who has been taking care of my nephew."

"An honour, my lord," the doctor replied respectfully, taking Julian's proferred hand and shaking it firmly. "But I merely oversaw Captain Wendover's progress—*amazing* progress that was accomplished by the assiduous care given him by Miss Clarke." The doctor nodded his head in deference to Miss Clarke, who was busily tucking Peter's blanket more snugly about his feet.

"The angel of mercy I wrote you about, Julian!" said Peter, bestowing a fond smile upon his benefactress as she straightened from her task. "I told you she was pretty, didn't I?"

Julian watched Miss Clarke's reaction to Peter's words and was surprised and pleased to note that she did not blush or simper, but rather assumed a patient, tolerant expression of neutrality. By this lack of consciousness on Miss Clarke's part, he was led to hope that her affections were not irretrievably engaged or that her ambitions were not depending upon Peter's partiality. Because of this, Julian felt safe in expressing his appreciation to her in rather warmer terms than he had at first dared. "I thanked your parents, Miss Clarke. But it seems as though I'm more in *your* debt than anyone's. I thank you, too, most of all."

Miss Clarke modestly nodded her acceptance of Julian's gratitude.

"You'll be even more in debt to her after she's nursed me all the way to Hampshire!" said Peter.

Julian felt his good humour severely tried at the thought of the possible complications which might occur if Miss Clarke continued to remain in Peter's company. And for some reason he found the idea of her close proximity in the carriage rather unsettling to his own comfort, too. It must be the boundless enthusiasm she exuded, and that damned loose bit of hair she kept tucking behind her ear!

But besides all that, Julian was nettled to discover that Peter had engaged Miss Clarke to serve as nurse on the journey without first conferring with him. Ruthlessly and coolly, he executed his initial thrust. "Lord, with all this indebtedness floating about, perhaps we ought to *pay* Miss Clarke for her exertions! It hardly seems fair to wrest her from her snug home in Kent and entrap her in a drafty carriage for two days without some restitution being made. What do you say, Miss Clarke? Will you allow me to pay you?"

"Oh, Lord! Now you've done it, Julian!" said Peter, rolling his eyes.

Undeterred, Julian cocked a brow, saying, "What can you mean, Peter?" But no explanation was necessary. Even if he hadn't already known that he'd succeeded in doing exactly what he'd set out to do—discomposing Miss Clarke—one look at the young woman made the matter sufficiently clear.

After blinking once or twice, as if she hadn't heard Julian correctly, Lilith Clarke's dark eyes met his with unflinching resolve. "You are all kindness to thank me, my lord, but I've only done as anyone would do for another human being. As for restitution, whatever contribution you wish to give to Mr. Hobbs, the chief patron and proprietor of the nearby hospice which houses so many of our wounded soldiers, would certainly be welcome. But *I* will not accept anything from you.''

Despite the soft cadence of her pleasant voice and the serene composure of her features, it was obvious to Julian that Miss Clarke was piqued. Eyes did not spark and crackle like a kindled fire without that fire being stoked. And her annoyance was justified, for he'd known very well that he'd offend her if he offered her money. He knew instinctively that she'd not want to be paid for nursing Peter, but rather drew satisfaction from the humanitarian nature of her duties. *That* realization was probably what had goaded him into being so damned vulgar! He mistrusted such generosity of spirit. It stirred up memories and feelings he'd as soon forget.

''I beg your pardon, Miss Clarke.'' Julian dutifully began his apology. ''I only wished in some way to show my appreciation.'' Besides, if he paid her, he wouldn't have to be personally beholden to her. To make his apology more acceptable, Julian resorted to a method of persuasion which had always served him well. He smiled. And if the tattle-tongues who carried gossip about London could be believed, there was nary a woman in England who could resist one of Julian's rare smiles. Humility demanded that he did not truly believe such an exaggeration, but he thought it worth a try.

"Certainly, my Lord Ashton," she said graciously, "you are forgiven." Yet despite her words, and though the kindled fire in her eyes had been tamped down to glowing embers, Julian could tell he still had fences to mend with Miss Clarke. The smile hadn't worked. It hadn't appeased her wounded sensibilities. He'd hurt her, and that made her seem vulnerable. Her vulnerability touched his heart a little, a fact that was disturbing and unwelcome. He felt a perverse determination to tear down fences rather than mend them. He said, "I'm surprised your parents approve of such a trip in the company of two bachelors."

Almost imperceptibly, she stiffened. "I shall bring along Janet, my abigail, as chaperon. My parents know Peter very well and do not fear—"

"They certainly don't know *me*, Miss Clarke," Julian stated implacably, "or they'd not be so willing to let you go."

"Good God, Julian!" cried Peter, rocking nervously in the chair. "You're going to give Lily a dashed bad impression of you! Really, Uncle, it's too bad of you to go on like this!"

"My point, Peter, is that while you trust *me* and I trust *you,* I think it peculiar and ill-advised for Miss Clarke's parents to trust anyone they know so little about. The world is not such a safe place as many people wish to believe."

"But how people choose to perceive the world is entirely their own business, don't you think, my lord?" Miss Clarke opined sweetly. "It has been my experience that one receives in kind what one gives out."

Julian was speechless, a condition in which he'd not found himself since he was six years old and his nurse had demanded to know if he'd been a greedy cow and eaten the last peach tart. At the time, Julian's mouth had been full and he'd been unable to answer without implicating himself. Otherwise, even as a child, he'd have come up with some suitable rejoinder. He'd always had a silver tongue, Richard used to say. And Tom had predicted that Julian's sermons would set the congregation aflame with good intentions. Empty words now.

Julian sighed, suddenly ashamed of himself for abusing Miss Clarke's (and her parents') philosophies, and forcing his own disillusioned views onto her notice. "I meant no criticism of your parents, Miss Clarke. You're right. How people perceive the world is entirely their own business. It appears we simply have differing ideas," Julian finally conceded. "Shall we agree to disagree in this case?"

"Of course, my lord," Lily returned, forcing a lightness into her voice. His words troubled her. Truly this was a hard, cynical man! But he'd been so happy to see Peter, had shown such a bounty of true affection at their reunion, that Lily found his expressed opinions and the apparent tenderness of his heart in confusing variance with one another. Perhaps he'd built a wall about his heart and admitted only his family within those impenetrable confines. What a pity if that were so! Lord Ashton had so much to give.

But she'd been tart with him, and she knew such behaviour was not what her papa would approve. Why Peter's uncle provoked her into such unseemly conduct was puzzling! She ought to pity him if he truly had so little confidence in the good in other people. He couldn't be very happy! But perhaps it was his slightly arrogant air that unsettled her. In Lily's estimation, all God's creatures were created equal, and she had difficulty understanding and tolerating arrogance. Then, covertly appraising his rather awe-inspiring presence, she decided that some people perhaps had more of an excuse for arrogance than others.

"We'll be travelling hours together in a closed carriage, my lord," Lily said at last, firmly pleasant. "We can exchange philosophies en route, and perhaps both of us shall be more enlightened by the time we reach Hampshire."

Lord Ashton smiled with faint contempt and bowed. Drat the man, thought Lily, he was being condescending!

Dr. Payne cleared his throat, startling Lily, who'd forgotten that the old gentleman was there, so caught up was she in her conversation with Lord Ashton. "It's more like *days* you'll be spending together, Lily. Peter must be able to lie down comfortably during the entire course of the journey and must be driven at a snail's pace." He turned to look at Lord Ashton and raised his bushy brows. "Did you bring a commodious vehicle in which to transport your nephew?"

"Indeed, I did," replied Lord Ashton. "A berline. And I brought a separate carriage for my servants and the luggage. We can drive as slowly as necessary, putting up at an inn one night so Peter can rest."

"*If* rest can be had at a roadside inn," groaned Peter good-naturedly, seeming glad the conversation had returned to a more congenial footing. "I'm desperate to get home and see Mother!"

"Your mother sent bedlinens to use on the trip, Peter, so you may wish to thank her for making your stay at a roadside inn a little more comfortable," Lord Ashton said, smiling warmly at his nephew. "Though I understand you're not as concerned with comfort as you used to be," he teased.

Peter laughed and shrugged a thin shoulder. Lily watched their friendly banter with pleasure mixed with pain. It seemed the viscount's affection for his nephew was the only thing that managed to warm the world-weary cockles of his lion's heart.

"We will not hurry at the expense of your health, Peter," Lily stressed, bending again to cover his feet, which were poking out from the bottom of the blanket. "I do not precisely understand the distance to your uncle's estate, but even *two* nights in an inn may be necessary to insure your safe passage." She turned to Lord Ashton for confirmation, sure of his cooperation at least in the matter of his nephew's well-being.

Lord Ashton quickly caught the meaning of her look and said, "Whatever is required to carry Peter safely home shall be done in a trice."

"In that we are agreed, my lord," said Lily, straightening and smiling with genuine approval.

"Indeed, Miss Clarke," he returned, inclining his head in a courtly manner. "In that, at least, we are agreed!"

CHAPTER THREE

THE MORNING NOT BEING far advanced, the doctor deemed it acceptable for Peter to begin his journey home that day. With an excited Janet's distracted help, Lily packed a small bag for the two of them.

In the parlour below, the vicar remarked on how frequently Janet's peg-leg could be heard knocking up and down the hall. Mrs. Clarke smiled indulgently. "Janet's dreadfully excited to be going on this trip," she said, twining yellow yarn into a ball while Shadrack, the black kitten, watched with singular interest. "That accounts for her pacing of the hall. The girl's never been farther than Dover."

"You do think Janet is sufficient chaperonage for Lily, don't you?" asked the vicar, lowering his morning paper from in front of his face to look doubtfully at his wife. "She's as young as Lily and not precisely as, er, *watchful* as one might wish a chaperon to be."

Mrs. Clarke tutted softly. "Do you really think Lily needs to be *watched*, dearest?"

"Well, no," replied the vicar. He lowered his voice. "But what about Lord Ashton?"

"He's an honourable man. I can see it in his eyes," Mrs. Clarke returned complacently, reaching over to pat her husband's hand. "And if something does go amiss, Lily's such a resourceful young woman I'm not at all worried about her."

"I've never known you to be mistaken about eyes, my dear," said the vicar, returning to his paper. "Therefore I shan't worry, either." And the subject was closed to both their satisfaction.

Julian's servants were fed hot beefsteak pie and cabbage soup in the kitchen, and were thereby well fortified for the trip, which, judging by the quickly darkening skies, seemed destined to be plagued by inclement weather.

Julian was induced to share nuncheon with the family while Peter napped, his insistence on greeting his uncle from the chair instead of the bed having tired him out considerably. Sitting at table with Lily, solemn, observant Rachael and their four brothers—ranging in age from eight to fourteen—proved to be quite an experience for Julian.

The children had undoubtedly been admonished to be on their best behaviour, and for this Julian was at first most grateful. However, since they were fearful of misbehaving accidentally, the chattering which would probably have taken place round the table was pretty much reduced to monosyllables and requests for second helpings. While he was used to eating alone and had not thought he would be likely to find entertainment in the conversation of children, Julian found himself wishing they would disport themselves in their usual lively fashion.

Midway through the meal, he was sorely tempted to break the tension by flinging a forkful of mashed potatoes at Mark, the bran-faced twelve-year-old sitting opposite him. This put Julian in mind of the schoolboy pranks he used to engage in with Richard and Tom, and he grew pensive.

"Thir?" said Rachael from her chair near the end of the table. "Why don't you eat your parthnips? Mama thays there will be no pudding for anyone who doth not finish hith parthnips!"

Julian laughed. This gave licence for the others to find amusement in Rachael's warning, and all of the children laughed with him. Julian noticed that Miss Clarke laughed, too, her brown eyes twinkling with merriment most attractively.

"By Jupiter," said Julian, fixing the little girl with a sapient eye, "I perceive you're the peacemaker of the family, Miss Rachael, always looking out after the other fellow."

"Takes after Lily," interjected ten-year-old Luke with a grin.

Julian winked at Luke, then returned his gaze to Rachael. "And I'm so glad you informed me of your mother's disinclination to serve pudding to people who have neglected their parsnips. I'm perishing for a slice of pudding!" Then he ate all of his parsnips, enjoying them much more in the relaxed atmosphere that now prevailed.

Fourteen-year-old Matthew, a horse lover, summoned the courage to enquire after his lordship's "sweet-goers," and eight-year-old John wondered aloud if Julian were very rich.

"*Very* rich," the viscount said gravely.

"As rich as Squire Winwood?" pressed the curious child, despite the speaking look Miss Clarke gave him. "He has an indoor water-closet, you know. Do you?"

Luckily, Mrs. Clarke called for the pudding to be served and the subject was allowed to drop. Fascinating as water-closets were, nothing could compete with a moist suet pudding.

THE BUSTLE of the port city of Dover was barely behind them when Peter fell fast asleep. It had been quite a trick carrying him from the bed to the elegant black carriage, which boasted a boot door and two side doors trimmed with silver and which was harnessed to four splendid greys and driven by a smartly liveried coachman and groom. The smaller carriage would carry Lord Ashton's valet, Pleshy, another coachman and groom, Janet, and the luggage, leaving plenty of room for Peter to recline in the berline.

They'd used a home-made stretcher to convey Peter, and his removal from the bed and out to the travelling coach managed to be practically devoid of the sort of jostling that made one sick. But, still, Peter had grown alarmingly white and pinched about the mouth by the end of the transfer.

Lord Ashton had brought some clothes for Peter, a smart forest green jacket and fawn-coloured breeches, but they hung and billowed about him, accentuating his emaciated figure. Besides the black greatcoat wrapped about him, which reached to the floor, he was also bundled in blankets. In his weakened condition Peter got cold very easily, and though the carriage was as snug as could be and not at all drafty as Lord Ashton had hinted earlier, and they each had a heated brick at their feet, every precaution must be made to insure Peter's health.

Even Lily was warm, though her grey wool redingote was probably half as thick as the viscount's greatcoat and her mittens were only of a poor quality. She wore a small-brimmed, unadorned grey bonnet and sturdy boots which were not in the least fashionable. Plain and simple, she thought, a smile tugging at her lips. She doubted that anyone so plain had ever sat in Lord Ashton's carriage before. Snatching a glance at the viscount only confirmed this conjecture. He was splendidly, though tastefully, rigged out in a Spanish-blue greatcoat with several capes, decorated with gold buttons.

Blankets were supplied for both their laps. They shared a seat opposite Peter and faced forward. Lord Ashton had arranged for the other carriage to precede them, so that any trouble with the road would be encountered first by the vehicle not carrying an invalid.

Peter insisted on sitting up while they threaded through the traffic of town, entertained by the scenes of everyday life he'd not been able to enjoy for weeks. A light flurry of snow fell, lending a holiday air to the sight of people treading up and down the pathways in front of the shops.

All seemed new to Peter, and the excitement of it and the removal from his comfortable bed wore him down excessively. Now his fair locks fell in a tumble over his eyes as he rested in a corner of the carriage which had been fortified with cushions, his complexion as pale as the linen covering the pillow against which he reclined.

Lily noticed that Lord Ashton watched Peter tenderly, concern showing plainly in his thoughtful expression. Moments passed with only the jingle of the carriage traces to intrude upon the silence. Lily gazed out at the scenery, which had become rather monotonous now that they were travelling past snow-covered pastures. She darted an occasional look at Lord Ashton and observed with dismay that he seemed to be sinking into a rather brooding appearance of melancholy.

"I could not believe it when your father and the doctor produced that stretcher." Lord Ashton broke the silence with the grim admission. "I had thought Peter would be able to walk to the carriage."

"He *can* walk, but he's terribly weak from lying abed for so long, and the doctor and I thought it would be best if he reserved his strength for the trip,"

Lily began seriously, wanting to be encouraging yet still truthful about Peter's limitations. "His muscles have become shrunken and stiff. He will need plenty of time to convalesce, and his exercise will have to be increased in moderate increments. He can walk into the inns when we stop—if he's up to it and if we support him. The trip will be exhausting for him, but he'll manage very well, I think," she said, wanting to end on a bright note. "Peter has great strength of will, you know!"

"You do not think we were precipitant in removing him from the vicarage, do you?" asked Lord Ashton worriedly. "I had thought that being home with his mother would help restore him to health sooner." He pulled his gaze away from his nephew for the first time in almost an hour, his expression indicative of the need for reassurance.

Lord Ashton continually surprised Lily. She had not thought he would require reassurance, or if he did, that he would admit to such a thing or, indeed, seek it from her. But then, she had not thought he would enjoy a meal with her rowdy brothers, either, especially after they had nearly run him down.

"It's always cheering to be tended by someone who loves you and is wishing and praying for your complete recovery," Lily readily agreed. She paused, debated inwardly whether or not she should speak of her empathy, then blurted out, "I know how you must be feeling, Lord Ashton. I have known Peter only a few weeks and it wrenches my heart to see him suffer so."

Lord Ashton once again turned to look at her, and Lily was pained by the suspicion she saw reflected in his face. Apparently, had she been inclined to be in love with Peter, she'd have found his uncle disapproving of the match. Though the Clarkes were from an old and respected family—her grandfather had been a baron—Lily supposed they simply weren't rich enough to suit Lord Ashton's notions of what Peter deserved in the way of matrimonial connections. Her father's living was comfortable and he had a small independence besides, but with so many children to feed, clothe and educate, it was forever a challenge to satisfactorily meet all of the family's needs. Lily suppressed a twinge of hurt and disappointment, and said proudly, "Do not think I've set my cap at him, for I haven't."

The hint of suspicion that lurked in Lord Ashton's golden eyes changed to appreciative surprise, as if he were impressed with her honesty. Much to Lily's dismay, she found herself enjoying such a look. But it was not of long duration. Once again his lids lowered to shade his eyes and he withdrew into a polite reserve. "What ever made you think I wished to hear such a confession, Miss Clarke?"

Lily's temper flared. "My Lord, I'm not a bufflehead! I easily perceived that you were concerned about Peter's, er, feelings for me. But you may rest assured that I have not, indeed I *will* not, encourage him!"

Lord Ashton did not react outwardly to her statement. Perhaps he thought it would be rude to clap his hands in delight! Lily turned to look at Peter again. In a calmer voice, she continued, "Often a patient is so grateful to his nurse, he thinks himself in love. But my affection for Peter is of an entirely different sort. He is one of God's creatures and—"

"You love all God's creatures, I suppose," drawled Lord Ashton. "Do you love the scoundrel who did this to Peter?"

"I pity him," Lily promptly replied. "One can only imagine what circumstances induced him to resort to thievery."

"Thievery *and* attempted murder," Lord Ashton corrected, in a voice that held not a trace of pity for the perpetrator of the crime. "You forget, Miss Clarke, the *pitiful* fellow clubbed Peter on the head and left him by the side of the road without a stitch of clothing to protect him from the bitter cold. He left him for dead. He meant to commit murder, but then I suppose you have a soft spot in your heart for murderers as well as thieves."

"I abhor the crime, my lord," Lily stated with feeling, "but I do not hate the criminal! If desperate straits brought him to thievery, even more desperate circumstances must have tainted his mind and heart to make him such a violent brute as to injure Peter."

"And how do you think such criminals should be dealt with, Miss Clarke?" the viscount asked derisively. "With kindness, with compassion, I suppose?"

Lily knew he was baiting her again, but she returned his disparaging gaze with clear-eyed conviction, and answered, "Every circumstance is different and must be dealt with differently. True murderers cannot be tolerated in society, of course, but in the case of thieves, sometimes compassion is called for. Joined with a firm push in the right direction and a willingness on the part of the criminal to reform, compassionate assistance of a criminal can sometimes completely turn his life about and make him an honest, responsible citizen."

"And if he is not, er, willing to reform?"

"A severe dressing-down, a thrashing, or incarceration are the other alternatives, my lord."

Lord Ashton surprised Lily with a sudden bark of laughter. Then, fearful that he may have disturbed Peter, he darted his nephew a concerned look. Satisfied that Peter was still sound asleep, he turned back to Lily and said in a low voice, "Good God, Miss Clarke, you're a cool one! That's an interesting creed you live by—'Love 'em first, but if that don't work, beat 'em till they repent!'"

Lily couldn't help the smile that teased the corners of her mouth. "That is not precisely what I meant, nor is it that simple. But there *are* people who are so hardened in their misconduct that the only way to reach them is to chastise them."

"That is something I would pay to see, Miss Clarke," murmured Lord Ashton, leaning back against the carriage squabs.

"My lord?" said Lily, puzzled.

Lord Ashton pulled the rim of his hat over his eyes and crossed his arms in apparent readiness for a snooze. "*You*, Miss Clarke. I would pay a tidy sum to see you delivering a blistering set-down to a hardened criminal. Yes, I would, indeed!"

Lily did not reply. She sat for some time, watching Lord Ashton's still-as-a-portrait profile. His aristocratic nose supported the brim of his hat, his lips remained firmly closed and did not quiver with the ins and outs of slumberous breathing. His chin jutted above his impeccable neckcloth in an unconscious gesture of stubbornness. His powerful arms were folded across his broad chest.

His outward appearance bespoke privilege, pride and implacable opinions. But Lily's heart stirred with compassion, because she had the strongest feeling that the elegant, unflappable exterior of this handsome nobleman hid within a great deal of disillusionment, confusion and pain. She wondered what life had dealt him to produce such steely armour to shield him from further distress.

As THE AFTERNOON WORE ON, the skies darkened increasingly and the sprinkling of light flakes turned into a full-blown snowstorm. Julian worried aloud that his coachmen and grooms would be frozen as stiff as pump-handles before they got to the next town, which was Kennington.

"And trudging through the slush and snow must be quite tiring for the horses," Miss Clarke added, peering out of the carriage window through the circle she'd wiped with her mitten. Julian had noticed how old and much-mended were her mittens. He feared her fingers must be as cold as ice. She had ought to keep them under the covers, but she seemed incapable of sitting idle for very long and was forever straightening Peter's blankets, or tucking behind her ear that errant curl of hers, or some such nervous activity.

"Yes, of course, the horses," said Julian, flashing Lily an amused look. "I had also been thinking of *them,* Miss Clarke," he assured her. "After all, they're God's creatures, too, aren't they?"

Peter, awake and alert after a long nap, said, "Don't roast her, Julian. She can't help being such a dear. She has a very kind heart!"

"An encumbrance which will make it deucedly difficult for Miss Clarke to travel through life without a great deal of inconvenience, I'm afraid," he opined lazily.

Peter frowned. "Never knew you to be such a sour philosophizer, Uncle!" He turned to Miss Clarke, who was sitting quietly with her hands—for once—still and clasped together in her lap. "He's not usually such a crusty fellow, Lily. I swear that sometimes he's downright amusing."

"Lord Ashton does not need to amuse me, Peter," Lily gently advised him.

"But neither does he need to be continually lecturing you about life and the pitfalls thereof!" groused Peter, perhaps a little irritable from the rigours of the trip on his weakened nerves. But whether Peter's nerves were frayed or not, Julian acknowledged to himself that his nephew was quite right. For some reason he was harping on ideas that he usually reserved for his own pondering. Miss Clarke just seemed so naïve that it would be a pity if someone didn't prepare her for those realities which were likely to crack the rose-coloured spectacles through which she viewed the world. But perhaps it wasn't his concern.

"I promise to stifle myself," Julian said carelessly. "I'm not usually such a jaw-me-dead, Miss Clarke. Ah, here is Kennington."

Yes, finally the outskirts of Kennington could be seen through the curtain of fast-falling snow. En route to Dover he'd stayed in Kennington at an inn called The Pig and Thistle and had found it to be (despite its name) very clean and comfortable for such a dwelling. Even the bedlinens had been aired, which spoke well for the efficiency of the inn's proprietor and made one feel reasonably sanguine about the cleanliness of the cutlery and dishes.

Julian had directed his coachman to stop there if they should happen to find themselves by first dusk only as far as Kennington. It was still an hour from sundown, but the snow was mucking up the roads to the point of becoming nearly impassable. He thumped on the carriage ceiling with his stick and the coachman pulled into the courtyard of The Pig and Thistle.

The weather being so reprehensible, the idea of Peter actually walking into the inn was not given more than a passing thought. He might fall in the slippery snow or, at the very least, be exposed to the cold and wet longer than would be prudent. Without a stretcher at hand, Julian decided that the best way to convey Peter into the inn was to carry him in his arms. Peter objected, his face turning absolutely crimson at the indignity of such a proceeding, and he staunchly refused to cooperate.

"Peter, don't be such a ninny," Miss Clarke advised him sternly. "If you're worried about looking unmanly or some such nonsense, I'll have you know that nothing impresses a woman less than the appearance of mulish pride. I know you're an out-and-outer when you're in health," she said bracingly. "You have nothing to prove to me or your uncle. We've only your welfare in mind, and want you feeling more the thing as soon as possible. But this can't be accomplished if you refuse to cooperate."

Peter bowed his head. "You're right, of course." Then, raising his head abruptly, he said, "But someday you'll see me strutting and as cocky as a rooster, Lily!"

Miss Clarke laughed. "I've no doubt of that, Peter. Now up you go and wrap your arms about your uncle's neck."

And so the thing was managed with nary another objection out of Peter. Julian had watched Miss Clarke's handling of the situation with interest and admiration. Truly she had influence with Peter, and her influence was improving his character. Carrying the light frame of his once-strapping nephew into the warm inn, Julian had the most disturbing thought that perhaps worse could happen to Peter than to make an alliance with an obscure vicar's daughter. But he determinedly thrust the thought aside.

"Lord Ashton," said the innkeep, a short, balding man with a face that had been ravaged by the pox, "ye're back, just as ye said! Will ye be wantin' the same room as ye bespoke before?" His eyes flickered over Peter, who had turned his head away in embarrassment, and behind Julian to linger for an uncertain moment on Lily. Then Janet and Pleshy appeared at the door, snow dusting their hats and coats. Janet had wrapped a scarf about the end of her peg-leg, probably to facilitate her walk from the carriage, made problematic by the slippery nature of the snow that sheeted the cobbled courtyard. Julian knew they presented an odd, discordant picture and probably engendered some colourful speculation in the innkeep's imagination. He decided to clear the matter at once.

"I'll need two rooms—a large one for myself, my nephew and my valet and another for my nephew's nurse and her chaperon."

The innkeep's deferential smile did not slacken, but there appeared a suggestion of uneasiness in his demeanour. Bearing the marks of one dreadful disease, he probably had no desire to expose himself to anything of an infectious nature. "Yer nephew is ill, then?"

"Ill, but not contagious. The war, you see. Please don't keep us standing thus in the hall, man," Julian said, his patience wearing thin as he sensed Peter's growing mortification. "My nephew requires a warm room immediately!"

The innkeep gave a start, made a deep bow and preceded them up the stairs. He led them to a room where a low fire was already burning and directly began piling more logs on the grate. "Now I'll go and make sure th' fire's built up in yer room, too, miss," he said, nodding to Lily. "When ye're ready, it's just next door."

"You may show my servant where it is," said Miss Clarke, indicating Janet, who still stood in the hall with Pleshy, the two of them talking and smiling like old friends. Julian noted that his valet certainly hadn't lost any time in becoming acquainted with Miss Clarke's comely abigail. And judging by the girl's giggling encouragement of Pleshy's much-practised charm, Janet wouldn't make a very attentive chaperon. She'd be forever in Pleshy's pocket. Indeed, it was the chaperon who most needed a chaperon.

Julian would have to be a flea in Pleshy's ear, tell him to refrain from seducing her. It would be cruel to saddle the poor crippled girl with a merry-be-got child. And judging by the vicar's propensity to harbour the unfortunates of society, the child would certainly become an addition to the prodigious quantity of God's creatures already residing at the vicarage.

Julian set Peter down on the bed and waited for the innkeep to shut the door behind him before he began to help his nephew out of his greatcoat. Peter brushed his hands away.

"By God, that was the most mortifying experience of my life! That innkeep ogled me as if I were some sort of weak-kneed cully! Now, do me the courtesy of allowing me to stand on my own two feet long enough to undress myself, Uncle!"

"Why, Peter," Miss Clarke began brightly as she stood at the foot of the bed, "even quite healthy gentlemen, like your uncle here, require the help of a manservant to get in and out of their coats and trousers!"

"That's different, of course! I feel so helpless! Away from the vicarage, I realize how ill-equipped I am to function in the actual world." He looked at Miss Clarke with a plea for understanding in his weary hazel eyes. "I'm trying to be reasonable, Lily, but—dash it all—having to be carried to my bed like a babe makes a man feel foolish!" Peter punched the bed with both fists.

"And apparently it puts a man in bad skin, too," said Julian repressively. Peter's response to this mild reproof was to cross his arms and clamp his lips together in the manner of one highly offended. Julian was on the verge of delivering a lecture to Peter about behaving more like a man and less like the babe he compared himself to, but Miss Clarke had moved towards Peter and now leaned down to bring her eyes level with his. Julian waited to see what she would say before he spoke hastily and risked upsetting his nephew further.

"I understand a little of how you're feeling, Peter," she said with quiet sincerity. "I do not presume to know *exactly* how you feel, of course, but when I broke my arm as a little girl and had to be fed and bathed and couldn't run and play with my brothers as I was used to doing, I became absolutely blue-deviled. The one thing that sustained me was my father's assurance that my arm would certainly mend, and that once it *did* mend I would appreciate its usefulness all the more and be exceedingly gay. I daresay it is very uncomfortable being an invalid when you have always been so active and vigorous, but I've no doubt that you will very soon be as strong as ever you were. Be patient, Peter, and let those that love you help you through this difficult time."

Peter raised his head halfway through Miss Clarke's bracing monologue and listened attentively. Now he smiled and cocked a brow. "Those that *love* me? Of whom are we speaking, Lily?"

Miss Clarke returned his smile but said dampeningly, "I was speaking of your uncle, of course!" She straightened up and moved to the door. "Now I must check on Janet and discover whether or not she's conceived the good notion of having the groom bring up our bag from the carriage! Then I'll find the inn-keep and bespeak you a nice dinner, Peter."

"Will you share it with me, Lily?" he asked her as she put her hand on the doorlatch.

"She may sit with you while you eat, Peter, if she wishes," Julian spoke up, struck with a sudden disinclination to dine alone. "But Miss Clarke will be having dinner with me in the parlour."

They both looked at him, surprise clearly writ on their faces. "Pleshy will keep you company while Miss Clarke and I are occupied. Then she'll be up willy-nilly to check on you, I'm sure. She can't be at your elbow every minute, you know. I hope you do not begrudge her a little relaxation?"

Peter frowned. "Of course I don't, Julian, but I never thought she'd find relaxation sitting at table with *you*. You ain't going to plague her with your gloomy prognosticating, are you?"

Julian raised a supercilious brow. "I may safely promise you that I shall not plague Miss Clarke in any way."

"Pardon me, my lord." Miss Clarke spoke up in dulcet tones. "I do not recall that you asked me to take dinner with you. Goodness, but my memory must be failing!"

"As well you know, Miss Clarke," replied Julian, sporting an equally honeyed smile, "I never asked you."

Miss Clarke bristled, obviously determined not to be ordered about by the likes of him. His smile broadened. "I'm asking you now."

Something flickered in Miss Clarke's eyes, something between irritation and reluctant appreciation ... for his audacity, he supposed. Despite herself, despite her disapproval of him and his cynical refusal to love all of God's creatures, she appeared to be on the point of agreeing to dine with him. Perhaps he presented a challenge. Perhaps the saint meant to help the sinner see the folly of his ways. What the sinner's motives were in inviting the saint to dine with him were most unclear to Julian, but he would not speculate.

Miss Clarke laid an index finger against her cheek and pursed her lips consideringly, as all the while her gleaming eyes hinted at a certain enjoyment in her power to refuse or accept his invitation. She probably had precious little experience with the opposite sex, though she handled herself very well despite this fact. "When do you mean to dine?" she finally asked him.

"At seven."

"In the parlour?"

"Yes."

"I'll be there. But you must put up with a rather drab little dress I stuffed into my portmanteau this morning," she confided matter-of-factly. "I haven't a lot of toggery, you know, and I chose it because it's warmer than most of my gowns."

"I shall contrive to 'put up' with it, Miss Clarke," Julian assured her. "Now do go and order Peter's dinner. I fancy he's sharp-set by now."

Miss Clarke looked a little abashed, as though she had indeed forgotten all about Peter and his dinner. She threw her patient a look replete with guilt and apology, smiled uncertainly, and swiftly left the room. Julian was still gazing at the door through which she had exited when he was recalled to the moment by his nephew's indignant voice.

"I'd never have thought it of you, Uncle, but having seen it with my own eyes . . . !"

Julian unhurriedly removed his greatcoat and draped it on a chair by the fire. "What can you mean, Nephew?"

"You were *flirting* with her! You were casting out lures to my nurse, *my Lily!*"

Julian "tsk-tsked." He bent to pull on Peter's sleeve, easing out first one arm, then the other from the heavy coat. "I don't suppose you noticed that the lady finds me quite hopelessly beyond the pale. I'm not in the habit of casting out lures to women that haven't the slightest inclination to like me, you know. A damnable thing, rejection. I don't court it."

Peter eyed him suspiciously. "Don't say she doesn't like you. All females like you."

Julian draped Peter's coat on another chair near the fire, then proceeded to go down on his knees to remove his nephew's boots. "Well, though she is decidedly female, Miss Clarke doesn't like me. Bend your foot, Peter. Dash it, where is Pleshy when I need him? Probably dallying with that chaperon cum coquette, Janet!''

Peter looked a little relieved by his uncle's offhand assurance of Lily's indifference to him, but upon further consideration of the situation couldn't help but express concern for another possible complication. ''It's all very well that she don't like you, Uncle, but do *you* like *her?*''

Julian did not reply at first, but busied himself with the task of tugging off Peter's tight-fitting Blucher boot. While Peter's girth had shrunk in size, his feet were as big as ever.

Did he like Miss Lilith Clarke? Julian wondered. An interesting question. Despite her stomach-disordering cheerfulness and affection for all of mankind in general—criminals not excluded—he had the most unsettling impression that he liked her rather well.

''She's not my sort, Peter,'' he told his nephew truthfully. ''Not my sort at all.'' Nor your sort either, he thought to himself. But now was not the time to broach that particular subject. Thankfully, at that moment Pleshy entered the room. Now he'd have the help he needed in getting Peter into his nightshirt and cap and tucked into bed where he could wait for his dinner in warmth and comfort.

Moments later, Peter offered Julian a repentant smile. ''I'm sorry, Uncle Julian,'' he said, yawning hugely. ''You must forgive me for being so suspicious. I'm taken with the chit, you see. When you feel that way about a lady, you think all other men must feel the same way you do." Peter's brows drew together. "We must talk about how I feel about her before we reach Ashton House."

"Of course, Peter," said Julian, undoing his neck-cloth in front of the mirror over the dressing-table. "But not tonight. I suspect you will need all of your strength simply to stay awake long enough to eat dinner. Is that agreeable to you, Nephew?"

A soft snore was the only reply.

CHAPTER FOUR

LILY STOOD AT THE PARLOUR window looking out at the courtyard of The Pig and Thistle. The mews were barely discernible through the veil of falling snow. The surrounding beech trees sagged under the prodigious quantities of heavy, white precipitation that nested in the branches. Lily couldn't remember such a storm in many years. One would almost suppose they were in mountainous Cumberland rather than in the mild shire of Kent.

Lily shivered and withdrew from the window, where each pane was laced with crescents of snow in the corners, to stand by the fire. The parlour was small and plain, with comfortable furniture scattered about and a good-sized dining-table placed against the inside wall. The cloth had been laid and the covers neatly set. A brace of candles stood in the middle of the table and the innkeep, or his wife, perhaps, had in lieu of flowers fashioned a centrepiece out of a bowl of nuts and apples.

All was snug and pleasant, yet Lily felt extremely restless. Usually when she felt this sort of half trepidation, half expectation, it was because she'd left something unfinished. She sat in a rocking chair by the hearth and, as she vigorously rocked to and fro, mentally relived the past two hours since they'd arrived at the inn.

No, she could not recall omitting some responsibility. She'd ordered Peter a light but nourishing dinner and had sat with him as he ate. He'd had a nap directly after Lord Ashton and Pleshy had undressed him and tucked him into bed, and had fallen asleep again straight after his dish of stewed plums and cream. He was quite worn out and had a little headache besides, so she hoped he would sleep soundly till the morrow.

While she'd sat with Peter, Lord Ashton and Pleshy had removed themselves from the chamber, but she could not imagine where they'd gone, since she could not picture his lordship hobnobbing with the locals in the taproom. Though perhaps that's where Pleshy had chosen to go to wile away an hour or two. Now Pleshy sat with Peter.

She had left Janet in their shared bedchamber, the girl being quite knocked-up from travel and excitement. Lily owned herself to be tired, as well, but buoyed by some inexplicable sense of adventure. An odd notion, since what could possibly be exciting about spending a quiet night in an obscure inn during a snowstorm?

"You count promptness amongst your list of virtues, I see."

Lily stopped her rocking and turned to observe Lord Ashton standing in the doorway. His tall, athletic frame filled the opening and his presence dwarfed everything in the room to inconsequential comparison. And while he could easily stun the beholder in a frowsy little parlour at The Pig and Thistle, Lily was convinced that he was fully capable of making just as great an impression in any drawing-room in London. Even the Prince Regent's.

"Papa taught us to be punctual," Lily replied rather timidly. She felt inordinately shy.

Lord Ashton stepped into the room. He was wearing buff-coloured breeches and a bottle green jacket. As always, his neckcloth was tastefully and impeccably tied. His hair shone like spun gold in the firelight. He fixed her with a penetrating gaze and a moment passed before he spoke. "Your papa has taught you a great deal." His eyes flickered about the room, then returned to her. "But I perceive that he has not taught you in the correct use of a chaperon."

"Oh!" said Lily, rising from her chair to stand by the fire, nervously chafing her hands behind her as if she were cold. Truth to tell, she *had* got a sudden chill. "Janet was fagged to death. I told her to go to bed."

Lord Ashton seemed to be assimilating this piece of information. He crooked one arm behind his back and pulled on his chin with the long fingers of his other hand as he walked slowly to the dining-table. "She cannot be of much use there, I perceive."

"No, indeed!" said Lily with a forced trill of laughter. "But I cannot help but feel the whole notion of *me* needing a chaperon is quite cork-brained! Don't you agree, my lord?"

Lord Ashton lifted his enigmatic eyes once again to her face, observed her with nonchalant purpose for a full moment, curled his lips in a mocking smile, and pulled out a chair. "Sit down, Miss Clarke. I'm positively feeble with hunger."

Lily did not think such a man could ever *look* feeble, however hungry he might be. And she did not suppose that lions of the jungle, to which the man was compared, looked especially feeble when they were hungry, but rather were more keen-eyed, cunning and purposeful in pursuing a remedy for their hunger. Lily sat down, and catching the sharp look in his lordship's eyes, felt suddenly as vulnerable as a lamb.

"You said I must put up with the toggery you brought on the journey, Miss Clarke," he said once she was seated. "But I find your gown quite charming. The rose patterns bring out the russet highlights of your hair."

"Th-thank you, my lord," Lily mumbled, blushing so furiously she was sure her cheeks were as russet-coloured as the highlights of which he spoke. It had been easy to shrug off Peter's compliments, but attentions of the same sort from Lord Ashton made her as flustered as a schoolroom miss, and her all of one-and-twenty! She supposed he felt it his duty to pay her a compliment or two. She would try not to let it discompose her.

Luckily the innkeep's wife entered just then with a selection of dishes. Apparently the proprietress of the establishment felt Lord Ashton deserved preferential treatment, for she brought the entire meal herself. Once the table was heavy-laden with numerous aromatic dishes, she left them alone. Silence prevailed while they both partook of the variety before them and proceeded to eat.

"Do you drink wine, Miss Clarke?" Lord Ashton presently asked, in a lazily teasing voice as he poured himself a scant amount of a pungent, fruity vintage into a tumbler. "Or does 'Papa' disapprove of strong spirits?"

Lily was slicing a sweet potato with knife and fork, her attention fixed on her task. She wondered if he would continue to enjoy a certain unholy glee at the expense of her vicarage rearing. She stifled her urge to retort something shocking. "Papa does not think wine is sinful in moderate doses," she finally replied in an even tone. "In fact, he drinks it sometimes to enrich his blood. But I prefer milk."

Lord Ashton set down the carafe and reached for the crock of milk, then poured her a glass. "Ah, your preference for such a creamy beverage must account for the milky smoothness of your complexion."

Lily's knife and fork fell from her fingers, clattering on the plate. She lifted her head and met his surprised look straight on. "Please, Lord Ashton, do not assume that, just because I'm a female, you must needs feel duty-bound to offer me compliments. I'm not such a fashionable one who regards flummery as my due. I am simply Peter's nurse and friend, and I would be vastly more comfortable if you would not comment on my person further. And you, I'll wager, will feel a heavy load lifted from off your shoulders. It must be fatiguing to have to cudgel your brain continually to come up with such *original* turns of phrase for every female whose company you happen to share.''

Lord Ashton laughed, which robust, delightful sound tickled Lily and made her smile quite involuntarily. "Lord, you offer me the word with no bark on it, don't you? Are you always so painfully honest, Miss Clarke?''

Lily opened her mouth to reply, but Lord Ashton lifted his hand, saying, "No, don't tell me. Your papa taught you to always speak the truth. Such a habit could be inconvenient at times.''

"As inconvenient as my trusting nature, I suppose,'' Lily suggested, placing a piece of roasted chicken in her mouth.

"Neither traits are conducive to surviving in this distrustful, dishonest world, Miss Clarke,'' he said, abruptly sober again. "But never mind that! I told Peter I wouldn't plague you with my cynical views. What I want to know—and I want you to answer with perfect honesty!—is firstly, why are you so convinced that my compliments are insincere, and, secondly, why do you suppose that you are not in need of a chaperon?''

Lily set down her fork and gave the question considerable thought. ''Well, firstly, perhaps I *do* have russet highlights in my hair—Mama and Papa have both said as much—and perhaps I have a tolerable complexion, but whether such attributes are worthy of comment is certainly up to the discernment of the observer. I'm quite sure you, my lord, moving as you do in noble circles, are used to being in the company of very beautiful ladies. If Leonard, the squire's son whose estate marches with the vicarage grounds, were to compare my skin to cream, I might believe him sincere. But from a viscount...''

Lord Ashton's brows raised expressively. ''I am at a disadvantage because I am a peer? I would be better believed if I were untitled?''

''You would be better believed, my lord, if you were less a man of the world and more simple—like myself.''

''And like Leonard, I suppose. I see. And the second part of my question?''

''I don't think I need a chaperon because I'm not a young girl anymore—''

''How old *are* you, Miss Clarke?''

''One-and-twenty.''

''A positive ape-leader!''

''Precisely. And besides that, I don't think you mean to seduce me.''

"I've not lived up to my reputation as a man of the world, then. All men of the world are seducers."

"Are they? Well, then you're not so much a man of the world as I had thought!"

"Such a pronouncement, Miss Clarke, quite takes the logic out of your answer to my first question. If I'm *not* a man of the world, you must believe then that my compliments are sincere!"

"Do you take your seat at the Upper House, my lord?" Lily enquired, impressed despite herself and disregarding his flirtatious assault on her logic. "You argue admirably. My brother Paul would find you quite fascinating."

"I don't recall meeting a Paul. Have you yet another brother?"

"Paul's a scholar at Oxford. He has aspirations for a public career."

"Hmm. This squire's son—Leonard, you say?— does he want to marry you, Miss Clarke?"

Taken aback at the viscount's persistent return to the original subject, and the frank question he asked, which was as direct as she herself might have phrased it, Lily answered laughingly, "Why, yes, he does!"

"When may I wish you happy?"

"You may not. I've no intention of marrying Leonard. He's a conceited popinjay. When he declared himself, he gave the distinct impression that he would be doing me and my family a great favour by marrying me."

"Was that the sole source of your aversion to the match—his manner of offering?"

"Heavens, no! I'm not such a noddy as that! I don't love him."

Lord Ashton grinned. "But I thought you loved all of God's creatures?"

Lily laughed. "Will you never stop quizzing me? You know very well that a certain sort of love is required between a husband and wife. I don't feel that sort of affection for Leonard. Indeed, I haven't yet felt it for any man of my acquaintance."

"Your circle of acquaintance is small," the viscount suggested.

Lily arched a brow. "I have gone to many assemblies in Dover. Papa does not disapprove of dancing, my lord. And perhaps we aren't quite the hermit-like, countrified society you imagine. Soldiers and dignitaries abound in Dover on occasion. It may even surprise you to know that I've received more than one offer for my hand!"

"I beg pardon, Miss Clarke, for having been so condescending."

Her eyes twinkled. "I forgive you."

"Somehow I knew you would!" he said. "By the by, it doesn't surprise me in the least."

"You have lost me, I'm afraid. What doesn't surprise you, my lord?"

"The fact that you've received several offers of marriage."

Lily flushed. "Spouting flummery again, I see."

"You forget, Miss Clarke, I'm not a man of the world, therefore you must believe my compliments no matter how uncomfortable they make you. But if you would prefer it, I won't pay you any more compliments for the duration of the trip. I promise."

Lily gave a sigh of relief. "Thank you! Your restraint would be greatly appreciated!"

They smiled at each other, and Lily found herself positively hypnotized by the warm expression in the depths of his strange golden eyes. She dropped her bemused gaze to the contemplation of her cooling plate of food and found she hadn't much of an appetite left. All that flummery must have unsettled her stomach.

Remembering her mama's advice about drinking milk to ensure a straight spine, she took a swallow, then lifted her table napkin to daintily dab at the corners of her mouth in case she wore a milk moustache such as her little brothers sported every morning after breakfast. As she performed this precautionary exercise, she kept her eyes averted to the floor by the sofa. Then she saw it—a fat rat as big as Shadrack the kitten boldly waddling across the rug. Lily loved rats less than any of God's creatures, including leeches. She screamed.

Up until then, Julian had thought the dinner going rather pleasantly. He had not found Miss Clarke's conversation to be at all insipid. She was open and confiding, honest to a fault, and absolutely refreshing. He had brooded in the coach all day about Peter's assailant and the perfidy of mankind, which mood did not encourage enjoyable chit-chat. Tomorrow, he had decided, he would draw her out even more. Though he knew she could not possibly stay so trusting and well-thinking of mankind—the passing years would see to that—in the meanwhile he would enjoy the unspoiled freshness of her personality. Maybe for a time—for the duration of the trip, perhaps—he could pretend that Miss Clarke would never change.

Now she was screaming, and for a reason not immediately discernible to Julian. The unexpected pitch and volume of her voice quite made him jerk, tipping the spoonful of pease-pudding he was guiding to his mouth so that it tumbled down his jacket-sleeve, leaving a puce-coloured trail in its wake. But when Miss Clarke thrust herself back from the table and stood on her chair, the flounce of her hem firmly clenched in both hands and held to mid-calf, Julian recognized the classic stance. Apparently there was a rat loose in the parlour. He stood up, threw his napkin on the table, and cast his eyes about the room, perceiving in his peripheral vision a long tail vanishing beneath the sofa.

Julian was about to send for the innkeep, feeling it not entirely seemly to chase a rat about the room himself, when said man appeared at the door, apparently alerted to the situation by Miss Clarke's vocal alarums.

"She spied a rat?" he asked Julian, his whole expression one of apologetic and agitated dismay. Julian nodded gravely, stifling his urge to laugh. The whole scene was amusing. He disliked rats as much as the next fellow, but they were sometimes part of the necessary evil attached to laying up at roadside inns. He had seen them before in otherwise very clean, estimable establishments. But if Miss Clarke only knew how she was exposing her trim ankles and shapely calves... "Don't fret, my lord, we'll fix that vermin in three shakes of a lamb's tail!" the innkeep assured him, turning round to exit the room and returning in a moment with a huge, drowsy-looking yellow tom in his arms.

"This here's our mouser! He'll make mincemeat out o' that rat," said the innkeep with military zeal. "He's as good as dead, he is!" And on this threatening note, he opened his arms and the tom fell to the floor. With expected feline aplomb, the cat landed on his feet, but this appeared to be the extent to which he was prepared to exert himself. Looking about the room with apparent bored disdain, the cat seemed to find nothing amiss and sat down on his haunches, lazily wetting one large, spread paw and bathing his handsome face.

"Ye blasted alley-beggar! Earn yer keep!" bellowed the landlord, waving his arms in a gesture meant to inspire the cat to movement. But to no avail. The tom was enjoying a leisurely toilette. His eyes were closed in pleasurable appreciation of his ablutions and he didn't appear near at all to being done. Now he was lapping away at the fluff of fur encircling his thick, kingly neck. If the great Sovereign Henry VIII had been reincarnated as a cat, he would be this one, thought Julian with amusement.

He slid a glance at Miss Clarke. She was still holding her skirts up, but her expression of fear was gone. She appeared highly diverted by the spectacle of the sublimely indifferent mouser and its lord and master, the irate innkeep. Her eyes sparkled with merriment and her mouth was upturned in a delighted smile. So, the little Clarke had an appreciation for the ridiculous. Julian had to admire her for that. Again his gaze slid down to the sight of her shapely legs exposed below her skirts. And he had to admire a pair of comely shanks like those, too.

Suddenly the skirts lowered. Julian returned his gaze to Miss Clarke's face to find her observing him with a defiant gleam in her eyes. She must have noticed his rakish perusal and was bethinking herself of one of "Papa's lectures" about the sin of lust, to be delivered to Julian at a more convenient moment.

"Blast ye, Sebastian!" roared the innkeep, reclaiming Julian's and Miss Clarke's attention. "If'n ye won't chase th' rat, there's no reason t'keep ye about the house!" Their embarrassed, near-apoplectic host, obviously at the end of his tether, left the room again, this time returning with a broom. He raised it above his head and spouted what amounted to a sort of battle-cry. "Out ye go into the snow and if'n ye freeze,

then it's no more'an ye deserve, ye worthless scavenger!''

At the upswing of the broom, Sebastian's attention
was finally caught. He lifted his head and beheld the
innkeep with apparent contempt, going so far, however, as to rouse himself to all fours and twitch his tail
back and forth angrily. This was no hen-hearted tom!

The broom descended, and so did Miss Clarke.
Down she hopped from her safely elevated platform,
saying with a plentitude of righteous indignation,
"Don't you dare hit that cat! Don't you *dare* hurt him,
or throw him out in this dreadful storm!''

The innkeep caught himself mid-swing and stared
at Miss Clarke in complete confusion. She stood before him, her hands on her hips, her feet slightly
spread in a somewhat belligerent pose. "What, miss?''
he croaked.

"I *said* don't use that broom on Sebastian, or I'll
return the favour of your callous mistreatment of this
magnificent animal by using the very same instru-
ment of torture on you!''

The innkeep lowered the broom to the floor, his
look of disbelief ludicrous. "How now, miss. Ye can't
be stickin' up fer this mangy tom. I've tried t'teach 'im
to run down the vermin fer a month now, but he ain't
catchin' on to th' notion, ye see! And I've punished
'im and kept back 'is food a mite, but still he
don't—''

"Do *not* tell me that you have beat this animal before,'' said Lily with ominous calm. Indeed, thought

Julian, the innkeep did not dare to admit to such a thing with such a wrathful avenging angel confronting him! It seemed Miss Clarke had completely forgotten the rat still loose in the parlour, and her fear of it, in the heat of her fervour in preserving Sebastian's hide. "I'll have you know, sir, that Sebastian is one of God's creatures and therefore undeserving of this sort of shabby treatment!" Sebastian appeared to share this view and showed his wholehearted approval of such a sentiment by rubbing himself against Miss Clarke's skirts.

"What do ye expect me t'do with 'im, then, miss?" whined the innkeep, cowed by the petite termagant. "I can't keep feedin 'im if'n he ain't useful about th' house. I'm not a rich man, miss, able to feed every stray what shows up t'my stoop. I've got nine chil'ren!"

Miss Clarke seemed affected by the innkeep's words and said, softening a little, "Well, and I perfectly understand that your first duty is to your children. However, I can't but think that if Sebastian isn't satisfactorily fulfilling his duties in your household, that instead of driving the poor thing out into the cold, you had ought, at least, to try to procure him another more suitable home. There is a lonely widow in town, perhaps, who would appreciate a companion?"

The innkeep made a scornful noise with his tongue. "Even a widow woman wants a cat what keeps down the vermin population. Just common sense, miss!"

Miss Clarke could not dispute this and looked worriedly down at the tom, who was now purring so loudly even Julian could hear him from across the room. "Are you sure he doesn't catch any rats? Perhaps he only does so when you aren't attending. I can't imagine that he could be so very *large* unless he eats a great deal."

The landlord sneered. "That one likes fish. He thieves it from the market whenever he can, and my kitchen ain't been safe from pillaging since he turned up. I would've tossed 'im out long ago if'n my lit'lest girl didn't take a fancy to 'im. But I can't keep 'im no longer, miss. I'll wait till th' morrow, but then out he goes!"

Miss Clarke had no reply to this, but her lips clamped together disapprovingly. She must have realized that while she could indeed keep him from tossing the cat out into the storm tonight, she would have absolutely no power to influence the actions of the man once she had removed herself from the premises. As she pondered this conundrum, the rat reappeared and fled for its life through the open door of the parlour into the hall, the innkeep scrambling after it with the broom. Sebastian watched this proceeding with feline smugness, then sauntered to the rug in front of the fire and stretched out for a nap.

Curiously, Miss Clarke did not swoon at sight of the vermin's mad dash for freedom; rather, she seemed to be wholly absorbed in a reflective silence. Julian walked to the parlour door and closed it, then turned round to find that Miss Clarke had lowered herself to the rug by Sebastian and was scratching the majestic fellow's head behind the ear.

Julian moved to a wing chair by the fire and sat. Miss Clarke presented a charming tableau with her skirts puddled about her, the hem pulled over the heels of her slippers, one arm supporting her as she leaned over the opulently furred, well-fed feline, her head bent and the flames of the fire illuming those russet highlights he had sincerely admired. Julian rested his elbow on the arm of the chair and cupped his chin, captivated by the picture of innocent domesticity she presented. Abruptly, she raised her head and met his bemused gaze with a troubled expression. He noticed that her eyes were also softened by the firelight to a warm, sherry brown.

"What's to do, Lord Ashton?" she asked him.

"What about, m'dear?" he enquired lazily, sinking into a state of comfortable good humour, brought on, no doubt, by a fine dinner, tolerable wine and the company of an amusing female who did not bore him in the least.

Miss Clarke's brows raised in surprise. "What's to do about Sebastian, of course. We certainly can't leave him to the mercies of that insensate innkeep!"

Feeling a twinge of foreboding invade his halcyon mood, Lord Ashton sat up in the chair. "Surely you understand the innkeep's disinclination to house a useless animal whose only ambition in life seems to be sleeping, keeping his handsome fur in fine trim, and dining at his leisure!''

Miss Clarke frowned musingly. ''Indeed, I do understand, but I can't help but think that Sebastian could be persuaded to share his load about the house if only he were treated with kindness and respect. And perhaps he's more of a farm cat than a village cat. Mayhap he pines for the country, my lord, and for a pasture full of field mice to chase and dine upon.''

Julian eyed Miss Clarke suspiciously. ''An interesting theory, but how do you propose to test it out?'' he asked her in a voice that pretended to be coolly unconcerned.

Miss Clarke sat up, unselfconsciously criss-crossing her legs beneath her skirt in the Indian style. She propped her elbows on her knees and smiled shyly up at Julian. The confiding nature of her smile was unexpected, and the little prick of happiness that it gave his heart was equally as surprising as unwelcome. ''Well, I have been thinking that perhaps we had ought to, er, take Sebastian with us! You have farms and tenants and such like, don't you, my lord? And somewhere on your vast estate, surely a cat might be useful to you! A capital idea, don't you think? And one that serves the needs of all!''

Julian, not being deficient in understanding, was not wholly unprepared for Miss Clarke's ''capital idea.'' ''Did it never occur to you, Miss Clarke, that I have already a surfeit of felines on my estate, and that they are all of them quite probably tough, wiry creatures whose useful mousing abilities make them emminently suitable for country life? If I were to introduce this fat, lazy fellow into their midst, they would frankly chew him up and spit him out!''

Miss Clarke's eyes widened. ''No, do you think so? His intimidating size might help him to insinuate himself into their ranks, however.'' She bent a contemplative look on the sleeping cat, whose huge head rested trustingly against her thigh. ''But we must at least give him the chance to prove himself. He could be taught to do better. If we leave him here, however, his fate is sealed! Why, I wouldn't even put it past the innkeep if he were to drown the poor thing! I would not be able to sleep for weeks for thinking of him, I promise you!''

Julian felt as though he were being carried along on a course not of his own choosing, rather like the irresistible force of a tidal wave. It seemed he had no choice but to agree to Miss Clarke's plan of rehabilitation for the miscreant feline.

''Far be it from me to be the cause—however indirect—of your insomnia, Miss Clarke,'' he drawled, ''or for the untimely death by drowning of this good-for-nothing cat, which, as well as being indolent, is a thief. I *despise* thieves.''

Apparently undeterred in her joy by the disparaging tone of Julian's voice, Miss Clarke rose up on her knees and leaned forward to avail herself of his hands and to clasp them in warm gratitude. ''Oh, thank you, my lord!'' she chirped excitedly, her cheeks aglow.

"You will not regret it! And you will be blessed for your kindness in helping out another of God's creatures!"

Julian liked the way Miss Clarke's small fingers curled round his larger ones. He liked the way she smelled, all lavender and rose-water. He liked the way her gown snugly accentuated the curves of her soft bosom and hinted at the smallness of her waist. But most of all, he liked the way her eyes shone with approval as she looked at him.

Then a thought suddenly occurred to him and dulled the edge of his happiness. "Pleshy has a physical intolerance to cats," he stated morosely. "Sebastian must needs ride in the coach with us."

Miss Clarke's eyes twinkled merrily. She sat back on her heels and concentrated on composing her mouth, which seemed inclined to tug the corners up into a smile. "I'm dreadfully sorry, my lord," she murmured unconvincingly.

"But not so sorry that you'd forget the plight of this slothful cat and instead employ your sympathies on my behalf, I suppose?"

"There can be no question that in this case, at least, the cat is more in need of my sympathy than you, Lord Ashton," she replied, then brimmed over with the laughter she had tried so hard to suppress.

Julian joined in her merriment with much unfashionable enthusiasm.

CHAPTER FIVE

AS WITH MOST DEVIATIONS from a man's accustomed behaviour, in the harsh light of early morning Julian's folly of the night before was brought forcefully home to him. Sated by a full stomach, his blood diluted with rich wine and soothing firelight, and beguiled by the diverting conversation and sherry brown eyes of a pretty female, he'd behaved most unwisely. Despite Peter's amused enjoyment at finding his uncle host to a stray cat, Julian could not be glad of his impetuous agreement to escort Sebastian to Hampshire, there to burden his servants with such a worthless addition to their menagerie of domestic dependents.

And his friendly behaviour towards Miss Clarke might be misconstrued by the young lady. Green girls from the country were sometimes wont to believe themselves beloved when they were simply being flirted with. But, Julian acknowledged to himself ruefully, the zealous little Clarke was probably more interested in his spiritual salvation than his marital eligibility. Nevertheless, from then on, he would take care that she was properly chaperoned. This step was probably as much for his own safety as for hers. There had been a time last night when he'd actually been tempted to kiss the girl. That would never do!

The day was cold and cloudless, the storm having blown itself out during the wee hours of the morning. But the roads were dreadful and their progress was trudging at best, necessitating a closed-carriage intimacy with Miss Clarke for several hours. Julian's inclination of the night before to encourage Miss Clarke's refreshing conversation he ruthlessly stifled. He sat in his corner of the carriage as mum and aloof as could be, leaving Peter to claim full possession of his charming nurse's attentions. Despite the strangeness of his bed and surroundings, Peter had had a good night, and his tongue was running like a fiddlestick, with him talking mostly about what he'd do as soon as he was well.

Except for a puzzled look that morning when Julian had returned her bright smile with a barely discernible one of his own and a prim, formal, "Good morning," Miss Clarke seemed to accept his change of mood with equanimity. She chatted in a friendly, unflirtatious manner with Peter, and, in the style of an excellent nurse, kept him comfortable and safe without offending him with excess cosseting. Though from *her*, perhaps Peter would not be as averse to excess.

As for Sebastian, he'd spent the first twenty minutes of the journey in Miss Clarke's lap, then suddenly switched his allegiance from his fair rescuer to Peter. After fixedly observing the animated invalid for the aforementioned twenty minutes, Sebastian slipped out of Miss Clarke's lap and onto the carriage floor, where he indulged in a leisurely stretch before jumping, in a trice, up onto Peter's seat. Julian was of a mind to remove the cat from his new snuggery behind the crook of his nephew's knees (Peter lay sideways on the carriage squabs with his legs slightly bent) but Peter claimed to be much flattered by Sebastian's favour and proceeded to encourage the cat's pretensions by scratching him between the ears.

Eyeing Sebastian, reclined so comfortably and with such a proprietary air about him, Julian again repined. "I hope he does not think to join you in your bed tonight, Peter," he remarked grimly. "That would essentially drive Pleshy out, you know, and Pleshy is not used to sleeping above the stables with the other servants. Alas, I've quite spoiled the fellow. I should be obliged to bespeak another room to accommodate my valet."

"Oh, that would never do!" Miss Clarke spoke up, horrified. "I would be quite miserable if I thought I'd caused you undue expense on this journey!" Her brow wrinkled and she added earnestly, "But then, you know, I cannot regret the saving of this animal from that horrid innkeep, either!"

"I'm sure you do not regret it, Miss Clarke," Julian replied equably, "but to be honest—you do like it when I'm honest, don't you?—*I* regret it heartily."

Julian was sorry for this damping speech when he saw the effect of it on Miss Clarke. She seemed torn between her concern for the cat and her natural disinclination to be a bother to Julian and Pleshy, or to be the reason for the expense of another room. No doubt her papa had taught Miss Clarke the virtues of prudence and thrift.

"Don't fret, Miss Clarke," he was compelled to say in a much kinder voice than he'd intended, but wishing very much to remove the worried crease from between her brows. "Hiring one more room would not bring me all to pieces. I'm not exactly purse-pinched."

"I'll say not!" agreed Peter. "Uncle Julian's got money to spare, Lily!"

"But not to throw away on a cat," Julian said drily. "I don't suppose it has occurred to either of you that regardless of Sebastian's preference for a room-mate, we could easily exercise our superiority as the more dominant, intelligent species of animal and, er, *compel* Sebastian to sleep where *we* choose for him to sleep?"

"Oh, you mean lock him out of the room? Yes, I suppose we could do that, too," said Peter. He looked down at Sebastian, who was blissfully sleeping. "Besides, cats are fickle creatures. By nightfall, he'll have tired of me and will be traipsing about after Lily again." Peter grinned at Miss Clarke. "And who could blame him?"

Miss Clarke smiled slightly, but turned her head to look out of the window, commenting on how quickly the snow was melting away and how dreadfully muddy would be the roads. Julian approved of the young lady's tactful neutrality to Peter's flirtatious sallies. She repressed him without offending him. That was not an easy thing to do.

Lily was hardly aware of the scene upon which she'd bent her gaze. As well as to discourage Peter's compliments, she had begun looking out the window as a means of disengaging herself from her fellow travellers. Her mind was full of thoughts and images that one night's unrestful contemplation had not been long enough to sort through. And it did not seem particularly odd to her that she should be thinking of Lord Ashton when she could, instead, be looking at him now or conversing with him directly. It did not seem odd because the Lord Ashton she was thinking about, the one she'd shared dinner with last night, had seemed a different person entirely from the one with whom she presently shared a carriage.

She had watched this same man carry Peter into the inn, the sight of his strong arms cradling his nephew a study in manly tenderness she'd never forget. The friendly conversation they had engaged in during dinner had made him seem genuinely interested in her uneventful life. He had drawn her out to speak of things she'd not normally discuss with a stranger—for, indeed, he was a stranger to her, despite what Peter had told her about his uncle. But the information Peter had related had referred much to Lord Ashton's public persona, not to his private person. Lily slid a glance at Lord Ashton, whose sharp profile bespoke the implacable nature of the man. Perhaps he hid his private self even from his family.

But then there had been that ridiculous scene brought on by the appearance of the cat! The memory of the fat rodent caused Lily to shudder, and at the same time chastise herself for possessing such a silly, sorry weakness as her fear of one of the least fearsome of God's creatures. But so it had been since she was a child. She could never abide rodents. She remembered how Lord Ashton had laughed with her over the absurdity of the situation, his features relaxed and warm. Now he had turned back into a marble statue, so beautiful to behold, but so cold. It was a pity, a great pity, indeed.

"I had never before noticed that Pleshy was intolerant of cats," commented Peter, yawning behind his hand, already tired after an hour's travel and ready for a morning nap.

"As a rule, I do not keep them nearby," said Lord Ashton.

"But, true to form, Pleshy has employed his charms to captivate Janet, I see." Peter nestled his head against a pillow and closed his eyes. "Forgive me, Lily. I'd as lief talk to you as sleep, but I can't seem to keep my peepers open. Daresay I shall dream of you, and that's better than nothing."

Lily watched as Peter's breathing became deeper. Within a moment's time, he was sound asleep. "Silly boy," she whispered with a sigh. "I'm sure he's been in love at least two dozen times already in his lifetime, and shall be in love again two dozen more at least!''

"You are wise, Miss Clarke," said Lord Ashton with indolent approval. She felt his eyes upon her and she turned to look at him.

"Am I? Perhaps if I were truly wise I would not allow Janet to be closed up in a carriage with your valet for hours a day! I was not aware that he was a reputed libertine. Do you think he'll make advances on her?" Lily looked speculatively about the carriage, scooting closer to the door on her side. "I think there's plenty of room in here for Janet, don't you? She's not very large and I should not mind a little squeeze—"

"But *I* should mind it very much," Lord Ashton assured her. "If I had thought there was enough room to accommodate Janet in this coach, I should have arranged for that from the beginning. She's your chaperon, after all, and the most proper of arrangements would have included her *constant* attendance upon you."

Lily gave a startled little laugh. "I suppose that's true! But I can't seem to become accustomed to the idea of her being *my* chaperon! Rather I begin to perceive that she's more in need of a chaperon than I!"

"That was clear to me from the start," said Lord Ashton with a certain smugness.

"Oh, you don't really think Pleshy would seduce her, do you?"

"He might." At Lily's dismayed expression, he relented a little, saying, "Don't worry. I've already ordered Pleshy to ignore the girl's obvious infatuation with him.''

Lily felt relief flood through her. "Oh, that was very good of you!''

Lord Ashton shot her a keen, sardonic look. "*Good* of me? Hardly! I only took what occurred to me as the most prudent course. I would not wish to put up with the girl's histrionics when Pleshy bid her farewell at Hampshire with not another idea in his head of ever clapping eyes upon her again.''

"Well, perhaps you were saving yourself some inconvenience, my lord, but at the same time, you prevented the poor girl a great deal of painful self-recrimination and a broken heart.''

Lord Ashton did not reply.

"She's already suffered so much in her short life, the poor dear,'' said Lily.

She turned again to look out of the window and was surprised when, after a few moments of silence and in an almost belligerent voice, as if his sympathetic interest had been piqued but he was loath to admit it, Lord Ashton said, "How did she come to be at the vicarage? What has she suffered, Miss Clarke? I can see she's lost a leg to accident....''

"Not an accident at all,'' said Lily hotly, always stirred to indignation by the recounting of wrong-doing in the case of Janet. "Janet was orphaned when she was but four years old. She had no relatives—at least none that would come forward and claim her when her impoverished parents died of fever—and she was naturally thrown on the parish. Not *our* parish, of course, for Papa would have dealt better by her, I'm sure, but she eventually ended up in a foundling home of the most wretched reputation! Papa learned of this home and the atrocities that took place there about a year ago, and paid a visit. By then, of course, Janet had become grown. She was working in the kitchen, tyrannized by a horrid woman who beat her and made her sleep in a corner of the pantry on a filthy bed of rushes not fit for a dog, much less a human being!''

Lily had to pause for a moment to calm herself. The contemplation of such ill-treatment towards a person made tears of anger smart in her eyes.

"What of her leg, Miss Clarke?" Lord Ashton prompted.

Lily had been visualizing that bed of rushes and imagining poor Janet shivering as she lay upon it all those cold winter nights. She blinked and focused her gaze on Lord Ashton, who was watching her intently. There was a concerned expression in the depths of those golden orbs that warmed her heart. Why could he not always be so kind, so "human?"

"She had contracted a disease as a child which affects the limbs. I daresay you've seen such afflictions amongst the beggars and poor of London?"

Lord Ashton's mouth compressed into a straight line. "Yes."

"The disease flourishes in the ragged ranks of those unfortunate people who have not the means to clothe themselves against the cold or to eat properly. Janet was chiefly affected in her right leg and it shriveled to skeletal proportions. Neglect brought on gangrene and the leg was amputated. Such would not have been the case had Janet been treated with respect and kindness.

"When Papa came home from the foundling home that night, I'd never seen him so humbled and distressed as he was by the sights he'd seen. It became his singular cause from then on to reform the place and its 'neglectful' patron, which is how Papa tactfully referred to the villain who owned that deplorable institution!"

"And he brought Janet home with him, I conjecture, to serve as your abigail?"

Lily smiled. "Yes, and I know what you're thinking—she is not suited to such a post. But I don't really require an abigail, after all! When I need help dressing, our chambermaid, Sally, does very well. But Papa was determined to give the girl a chance to prove herself capable of doing something besides scrubbing out pots. He pitied her excessively, you see."

"Yes, I see. Do you think Janet has promise as an abigail, then?"

Lily chuckled and shook her head. "What Janet's talents may be, I've yet to discover," she admitted. "She's a very good-natured girl. I expect that her happiness in finding herself amongst people who do not ill-use her has made her spirits rather high. At any given time, one might find her romping with the children, examining with delight the feathery perfection of a dandelion, or doing cartwheels in the hall!''

Lord Ashton smiled. "I can well imagine her gratefulness at the change in her circumstances."

Lily grew sober. "It is more than gratefulness. Janet had been but barely existing before. Simply put, in the past year she has begun to truly *live*. And we all know what abundance life has to offer to those who have the health and strength of spirit to enjoy it. All those little things, you know."

Lord Ashton pursed his lips and said acidly, "Ah, yes! The *little* things. Sunsets, a child's laughter, et cetera."

Lily was not daunted by his mock and answered with characteristic facility. "Maudlin and trite, you are thinking. But I'm not ashamed to admit that I feel you are teasing me about the very sort of things that *do* make life worth living."

"I should rather think a spanking team and a well-sprung carriage, being beforehand with your tailor, and able to command at least some of the more elegant creature comforts would be more effectual in making life worth living. Seems to work for most of my friends."

"Don't take me for a gudgeon, Lord Ashton. I do not scorn the niceties of life you refer to. Yet I still believe that your friends cannot truly enjoy such niceties if they become immune to the simple pleasures—like a child's laughter."

Lord Ashton did not reply. His lips were rather tightly compressed and his eyes were averted. She thought she may have gone too far, and wishing to stay on speaking terms with Peter's uncle for all their sakes, she said, "Goodness, just listen to me! I beg your pardon, Lord Ashton. I did not mean to lecture you! I'm persuaded that you do not wish to exchange philosophies. I promise you I will sit mumchance till we stop for nuncheon."

Lord Ashton bowed his head in mute acceptance of her apology. She prepared herself for an uncomfortable, protracted silence, so was greatly surprised when he turned to her with a rather friendly expression in his eyes, saying, "You learned all that cant from your brother Paul, who brought it home from Oxford, I suppose. Does Papa approve, Miss Clarke?"

"No, indeed, my lord," Lily admitted sheepishly. "But then, I'm not perfect. That would be so boring, don't you think?"

"Exactly my thoughts on the matter," Lord Ashton returned gravely. "I knew you and I could come to agreement on *something!*" Lily was sure she perceived a rather wicked twinkle in his eyes before he tipped the brim of his hat down to cover them and leaned back into the squabs for a nap. Silence reigned within the carriage for several moments, and Lily thought it would indeed continue this time till they'd reached the destination they'd decided upon for the partaking of the noon meal. But it was not to be. The carriage lurched to an abrupt stop, waking Lord Ashton, Peter and Sebastian from their respective snoozes.

Sebastian, caught unawares while he purred happily through a fishy dream, was projected into the air and onto the floor. To his credit, though his fur certainly stood on end, he did not yowl. Peter would have quickly landed on top of the cat if his uncle had not handily caught him mid-tumble. "What the deuce?" Peter exclaimed, his wide-opened eyes still fogged with sleep.

"Don't panic, Nephew," Lord Ashton reassured him, leaning forward to straighten Peter's blankets. "We've stopped for some reason. Probably the other carriage is mired in a muddy rut."

Lily, not easily put into high fidgets (except in the presence of a rodent), calmly pressed her face against the window glass to see what she could see. She came nose to nose with the groom who'd been riding on the box with the coachman. She bashfully drew back, as did he. Standing at attention, he rapped ceremoniously on the carriage door.

"Yes, Bob?" said Lord Ashton. "What's the matter?" Lily noticed that while he spoke in a calm manner to the groom, Lord Ashton looked uncommonly rigid and alert, and had reached inside his greatcoat pocket with deliberate intent. But his hand remained inside and appeared to be balled into a fist, or perhaps clutching something. Lily was curious and, despite herself, faintly alarmed. It appeared that Lord Ashton carried a weapon on his person!

The groom, a freckle-faced young man with a shock of red hair that protruded from beneath the brim of his three-cornered hat, opened the door marginally so as to keep the cold air out, and stuck his pink nose inside. "There's a gig orf the road, milord. The coachman o' the forward carriage stopped t'lend a 'and. 'E knew that's what ye'd want, milord, but 'e sent me down t'ask ye, what with the cap'n aboard an' all, if'n ye'd rather go on and leave 'em to Prov'dence."

"How nice of Bertram to ask my permission," drawled Lord Ashton. "I suppose he's already off the box and digging the unfortunates out from a snowdrift, or some such thing?"

"Yes, milord, 'e is," admitted Bob with a grin. "Bert, 'e knew what ye'd say, milord. 'E didn't need t'ask!"

Lily listened to Bob with interest. So Lord Ashton's servants took it for granted that their master would never pass a mishap on the road without lending assistance. This spoke well for the viscount's inherent "goodness," whether the notion suited him or not.

"How depressing to be so well understood by one's servants," commented Lord Ashton. "I suppose you made certain that nothing about the accident appeared havey-cavey? Have you got your weapons about you, Bob? Sometimes the most innocent scene can be a façade for, er, ulterior motives."

Bob waved a large pistol in front of the window. "Yes, milord. Me barkin' iron is loaded and ready!

But the cub don't look shady t'me, jest a mite young and stupid, I'd wager. 'Pears 'e run orf th' road fer no reason what's clear t'me. There's a chit with 'im, and she's givin' 'im pepper, she is! Kickin' up dust t'blind ye, milord!''

"A woman?" Lily spoke up. "And you say she's distressed?"

Bob shifted his gaze to Lily and ducked his head respectfully, a furtive hand movement indicating that he wasn't sure whether or not to remove his hat. Since it was much too cold to be outside with an exposed scalp, Lily was glad when he decided to keep it on. "Yes, miss. In the boughs, she is," he cheerfully reiterated. "Can't ye hear 'er caterwaulin'?"

Indeed, now that he mentioned it, Lily did hear some discordant noise in the background. She immediately grew suspicious that the woman might need assistance of a rather different nature than the righting of her carriage. "I had better go and see if there is something I can do for her," said Lily, throwing off her lap-rug.

"My dear Miss Clarke, I can't conceive of one good reason why you should leave your warm carriage to run to this woman's aid," Lord Ashton began repressively. "From Bob's account, I must conclude that she is in no way harmed, only nettled. And if she is angry with her companion, you can be sure it's because she feels it entirely his own fault that they are in their present predicament."

"Sounds logical to me, Lily," Peter agreed, rubbing his eyes sleepily. "Man and wife having a tiff."

"Well, and so it may be," admitted Lily, wrapping her scarf more securely about her neck in anticipation of the brisk winter air outside the carriage. "But if she is needful of something else, she is more apt to confide in another woman." Lily reached for the door handle and was greatly surprised when Lord Ashton covered her hand with his. The feel of his warm palm and the sight of his strong, tapered fingers closed over hers sent a ripple of awareness up her arm. She lifted her startled gaze to his. The Lion's eyes, fixed upon her as they were and at such close proximity, were mesmerizing.

Julian was momentarily arrested by the shy hesitancy in Miss Clarke's expressive brown eyes. The girl was so damned genuine, and it was apparently impossible for her to hide her honest and immediate reactions. He had flustered her by touching her—yes, he'd felt that shiver!—and he'd done so without meaning to, without any flirtatious intentions whatsoever. But the delicate colour that rose to her cheeks made the idea of a flirtation rather appealing. Too appealing. He suppressed such a horrendous notion by reminding himself that she was a meddlesome do-gooder, and that she was, at that very moment, determined to meddle and do good in a situation where her interference would very likely not be appreciated. He removed his hand.

"I cannot physically bar you from leaving the carriage," he coolly began, assuming a look of indifference. "You are not a servant of mine who can be ordered about, nor are you related to me in any way, which relationship would grant me the freedom to exercise a bit of authority in your behalf—for example, to save you from doing something . . . foolish."

He watched her stiffen. He saw her eyelids lower in embarrassment or anger, he wasn't sure which. There was a pause while she gathered her composure, and then she finally lifted her gaze to meet his. Her small chin jutted defiantly. The soft, shy look in her eyes had been replaced with fiery determination.

"If you consider it foolish to try to discover if you can be of service to another human being, then I *will* be foolish," she told him flatly. She pushed open the door and stepped out. Bob, all agog with watching the Quality spar, jumped quickly out of the way. "Besides," she said on a parting shot, "I don't understand why you're making such a fuss over what *I'm* doing, when it doesn't seem any different to me than what *you're* doing by assisting them with their carriage!"

"The difference, Miss Clarke," Julian retorted, control over his own temper slipping away, "is that I am not prying into their private affairs! Helping to right a carriage that is off the road in a snowdrift is quite a different matter than playing a self-elected referee in the middle of a marital boxing match! I only hope the lady does not land you a facer!"

Miss Clarke "humphed" over her shoulder and stomped away through the snow.

"Zounds, Uncle," Peter ejaculated, his sleepy eyes now fully alert. "Never before heard you raise your voice to a lady!"

"I never—" Julian began loudly, then in a much quieter tone repeated, "I never raised my voice to her." He leaned back into the squabs and crossed his arms.

"Beg pardon, Julian, but you did!" Peter insisted, grinning. "She's a feisty little baggage, I'll admit, but it's in her nature to—"

"Put herself in the way of danger," Julian snapped, gritting his teeth. "Miss Clarke's trusting nature may someday get her so deeply in the suds, not even those innocent brown eyes of hers . . . !" He released a hiss of frustration. Leaning over to look out of the window, he craned his neck to try to catch a glimpse of the carriages ahead without letting down the glass and sticking out his head in so obvious a manner. "I suppose I must get out and sully the shine of my boots in this damnable snow! Pleshy will sulk tonight as he restores them to their original luster. But I dare not leave the little shatterbrain to her own devices!"

"Julian!" said Peter, laughing. "You're making much to-do over nothing! Surely the worst that could happen is that they will tell her to mind her own business!"

"You are mistaken, Nephew. Much worse could happen." This comment silenced and sobered Peter, so Julian tried to reassure him with a smile. "Don't fret. I'll take care that nothing happens to her. You go back to sleep. Here's your cat! At least the considerable amount of warmth this fat, furry fellow emanates partially repays us for keeping him." He picked up Sebastian, who was still a bit tetchy from being thrown from his berth, and placed him in the circle of Peter's arms. "Use him for a muff," he advised before he let himself out of the carriage and shut the door quickly behind him.

The air was quite nippy and a chill breeze struck him in the face as soon as he stepped past the lee side of the carriage. The coach that carried Pleshy and Janet was just a few feet ahead. And farther up the road was the unstable vehicle in question, its front left wheel sunk up to its top spoke in slushy snow. It was an unprepossessing gig with a tattered leather hood. His servants were digging industriously to free the wheel, after which they would have to inspect it to ascertain if it was still roadworthy.

The tall, muscular, ruddy-complected fellow in the simple yeoman's garb who was assisting them in this effort was, no doubt, the driver of the gig. Julian observed that he was no more than a lad—perhaps eighteen or nineteen by quick estimation—and his help in digging out the wheel was intermittent, due to the necessity he felt in replying to the constant barrage of recriminations being flung at him by a ginger-haired girl of about sixteen who ranted at his elbow. What the girl was saying was indecipherable to Julian, for she spoke with the speed of a hummingbird's wings. Miss Clarke stood quietly at the termagant's side, her hands clasped demurely together, as if waiting for a lull during which she might throw herself into the fray.

As Julian passed his forward coach, he glanced in at the window and saw Pleshy and Janet watching the arguing couple with shared amusement. Pleshy's dark, Gaelic head was bent close to Janet's fair one, and he was apparently saying something quite pithy, or, perhaps, tickling her ear with his warm breath, or, perhaps, both.

Julian stopped for a moment and frowned reprovingly at Pleshy. Pleshy at first looked startled and chagrined by Julian's unexpected appearance, then his keen valet's gaze dropped to his lordship's boots and back up to his lordship's face in an expression as eloquent of reproof as Julian's. Julian shrugged with aplomb in answer to his valet's silent reprimand for water-spotting his boots, shook his finger at him as a reminder of his own reprimand, and walked determinedly towards Miss Clarke.

That lady was no longer standing demurely on the periphery of the quarrel. She was nodding her head understandingly as the teary-eyed girl poured out her heart to her in language which Julian still could not translate into the King's English. The chit was very pretty, plump and rosy and dressed in a fustian round gown and a worn wool cape. Behind them stood the girl's burly companion, looking cross as crabs.

Julian had a rather sick feeling in the pit of his stomach. He'd a strong suspicion that his role as Good Samaritan was about to expand to alarming proportions. Either that, or he was about to have his cork drawn by a strapping farmer with forearms the size of milk jugs!

CHAPTER SIX

"YOU'RE GOING TO HAVE TO slow down and speak more clearly," Miss Clarke was saying to the near-hysterical girl. "I've plainly heard and understood only part of what you've told me so far, and I do so want to comprehend your situation completely!" Julian was relieved to know that he wasn't the only one who thought the young chit's speech resembled gibberish.

Judging by the youthful appearance of the duelling duo, Julian concluded that they were probably newlywed and having their first spat. He folded his arms and stood silently watching while Miss Clarke attempted to calm the girl by placing a gentle hand on her arm, smiling pleasantly and speaking in a reassuring manner. Presently the girl did respond to these tactics. Her diatribe ceased, her shoulders sagged and she heaved a great sigh.

All the while her husband also watched, but his expression was venomous. Rather like being in the presence of a snake posed to strike, Julian felt that to avoid being attacked by the sturdy built lad, his best course of action was to take no action at all, and certainly make no sudden movements. He wasn't afraid of the outcome should he be compelled to defend himself, rather he was averse to the idea of wasting his time in a senseless rough and tumble and ruining his clothes in the snow.

After all, he'd nothing against the fellow. He didn't even know him. And they wouldn't be eyeing each other so circumspectly now if Miss Clarke hadn't decided to stick her nose in where it didn't belong. They were strangers and would have remained strangers had Miss Clarke minded her own business. And in Julian's opinion, keeping most of mankind at arm's length and in the safe category of "stranger" suited him just fine, thank you very much.

The man swung his shovel across his massive shoulder and stepped forward. Scowling lines of disapproval were carved in his broad forehead from right to left temple. He stood next to the woman and stared hard at Miss Clarke. "Don't put yerself t'trouble, miss, listenin' t'Belle's whinin'. There be nothin' wrong with her what a good dinner and a night's sleep won't cure. She's just a mite fidgeted by the mishap."

In response to this belittling description of her anguish, the young woman turned on her companion and exclaimed, "Brute!" after which she burst into tears and flung herself against Miss Clarke's bosom. Miss Clarke obligingly wrapped comforting arms about the strange girl and patted her back while she had a hearty cry.

Rather than falling into a rage over the unflattering name with which his companion had dubbed him, the lad's face drooped pathetically. He seemed genuinely disturbed by the girl's sobbing. This encouraged Julian sufficiently to take measures in bringing this Cheltenham Tragedy to a speedy conclusion. Naturally, to accomplish this task, he would deal with the less emotional of the couple.

"I'm Lord Ashton," said Julian, stepping forward with a friendly smile and extending his hand to the young man. "You may well rue the moment we discovered your accident on the road. Certainly another coach would have come along to assist you by and by."

The lad eyed Julian suspiciously at first, then, perceiving that Julian was quizzing him in a good-natured sort of way, his frown relaxed a little. He, too, stepped forward, and after he'd wiped his palm on the rough fabric of his trousers, shook hands.

"Jasper Tupper. Me and my sister, here, is bound fer Kempe's Corner."

"Your sister, eh?" Julian glanced at Miss Clarke, who, not unexpectedly, smiled triumphantly back at him from over Miss Tupper's heaving shoulders. Apparently he *had* jumped to conclusions in supposing that the tiff was between a husband and wife, but, in Julian's estimation, there really wasn't much difference between a sibling quarrel and a marital one. Neither should be interfered with, unless of course there was violence involved. In this case, the only violence seemed to be in the intensity of Miss Tupper's unhappiness.

"Aye. She's t'be married at week's end," Jasper replied bluntly and in a slightly belligerent tone. This statement, which was apparently heard by Miss Tupper despite her noisy sobbing, brought on an even louder outpouring of grief.

Julian raised a speculative brow. "Indeed! She does not seem, er, *happy* about the arrangement."

"She is very *un*happy about it, my lord!" Miss Clarke spoke up. "That much, at least, I was able to gather from her conversation earlier. But I became confused when she began to speak of wooden teeth and rheumatism! I only supposed she was concerned about her father."

"Oh, I wish't that were true!" wailed Miss Tupper, momentarily lifting her teary face from off Miss Clarke's shoulder to clear up the misunderstanding. "Pa's dead, and our mum, too. Jasper takes care o' me now, but he's got some henwitted notion in 'is noggin that I ought to marry Old Man Grampton, the butcher of Kempe's Corner! It's my husband-to-be what's fallin' apart from old age!" Then she resumed her crying as before.

"Ah, a marriage of convenience," said Julian.

"And a disgusting business it is, if that's true!" exclaimed Miss Clarke, the familiar spark of righteous indignation igniting in her eyes. "No one should be made to marry where there is no love! And in this case, where there is a vast difference in ages, to force such a union would be criminal!'' She turned to Jasper, who was cringing and miserable. "How can you do this to your sister? How can you be so heartless?''

Completely cowed, Jasper hung his head and did not respond.

"Well, Mr. Tupper?" prompted Miss Clarke. "Have you no defence for your actions?''

Julian took pity on the hapless Jasper and said, "Perhaps Mr. Tupper was simply looking out for the welfare of his sister by arranging a suitable marriage.''

"No marriage is suitable if either of the parties in question do not hold the other in affection,'' Miss Clarke insisted. "There can be no excuse for coercing this girl into nuptials which are abhorrent to her!''

Jasper's head reared up. His countenance had reddened considerably. "I'm jest a poor tenant farmer, miss, tryin' t'make a livin'. Belle don't have no dowry ner settlements fixed on 'er, but Old Man Grampton didn't ask for nothin'. Belle'd have nice things if'n she married 'im—pretty gowns and such. Stayin' with me, she's got nothin' and won't never have nothin'!''

"Oh, don't blame Jasper!'' exclaimed Miss Tupper, unexpectedly rushing to the defence of the brother whom she had moments earlier called a "brute." She pulled away from Miss Clarke and commenced an unproductive search through her pockets for a handkerchief. Miss Clarke threw Julian a beseeching look, and, after some mental debate, he plucked his own monogrammed handkerchief from his inner waistcoat pocket and handed it with a sigh to the groping Miss Tupper.

She dried her tears and calmed herself, saying, "Jasper can't help it! He's so determined that I won't go t'work at the inn nearby, ner at the squire's house! He says the men there are all *libertines!* And seeing as how I'm a well-looking girl," she confided with a blush, "they'd try t'have their way with me! He thinks the best thing for me is t'get shackled t'some well-blunted gent. So when Mr. Grampton made an offer fer me, Jasper leapt at it in a pig's whisker! But I'd rather work in the kitchen as the lowest scullery maid than marry that wrinkled, leerin' ol' butcher! He's got a stomach as big as a kettle and no hair on his head besides! Oh, I can't bear it!" Miss Tupper dissolved into tears and blindly staggered forward, till she collided with Miss Clarke and once again availed herself of a soft shoulder to cry upon.

"Have no other men offered for your sister's hand, Mr. Tupper?" Julian enquired. "A *younger* man, perhaps?"

"Aye, they have," admitted Jasper. "But she don't favour none of 'em, and I thought if'n she was goin' t'marry someone she don't love, she might as well tie the knot with some cove what's warm in th' pocket, so t'speak."

"That's very true," Julian said agreeably. "But if she would rather make her way in the world, working somewhere, you know, I should not discourage it if I were you. She might be happier in an independent situation where she earns her own money, than married to a man she, er, dislikes, even though she might have all the wealth in the world at her disposal.''

Jasper appeared to be considering this. ''You *could* be right, milord. But hereabouts there's no place t'work what's safe fer a comely chit like Belle. I've seen as how the men from Collinwood House leer at 'er, and as fer that innkeep at The Pig and Thistle...! Well, I know *his* sort, milord! He can't be trusted as far as ye kin throw a horse!''

''I thought as much!'' opined Miss Clarke. ''Anyone who beats cats and throws them into the snow! Wicked, utterly wicked!''

At Jasper's puzzled look, Julian explained, ''We put up there last night. Rescued a cat. Quite a lazy, useless fellow, but one of God's creatures, you know. But never mind that! What's to do about your sister?''

As soon as the words were uttered, Julian was ready to kick himself. It was an appalling thought, but it appeared that Miss Clarke's penchant for meddling was rubbing off on him! It was certainly no business of his how Jasper dealt with his little sister, but, still, it was rather too bad for the girl to be married off to a grizzled old man, and a butcher at that, when she could hold a nice position as a servant in a respectable household where good servants were valued.

At Ashton House, for example, the servants enjoyed a camaraderie amongst themselves that resembled the affectionate ties of a large family. And Belle's chances for marriage would increase, since there would be a whole new county full of young men for her to meet and perhaps be courted by. He wondered if Mrs. Strand, Ashton's housekeeper for some thirty years now, could use another chambermaid.

Suddenly he said, "Miss Clarke, do I look flushed?"

Miss Clarke blinked and answered, "No, my lord." She tilted her head to the side. "Though your nose is a little pinkish. The tip is quite cold, I daresay. Why do you ask if you're flushed? You're not falling ill, are you?" Did he imagine it, or did Miss Clarke's eyes register concern?

Julian rubbed the tip of his nose with his gloved hand and reminded himself that Miss Clarke felt a measure of concern for all of God's creatures. The worried look in her eyes just now when she enquired after his health could have been just as easily inspired by a dog with a thorn in its paw. "I'm suffering from deliriums, I'm afraid."

Jasper frowned, Belle lifted her teary face from off Miss Clarke's shoulder to stare curiously, and Miss Clarke looked as though she weren't sure whether to smile or scold. "Deliriums, my lord?"

"You know—confusion, disordered speech, hallucinations, that sort of thing."

The Tuppers looked alarmed, and Belle even went so far as to disengage herself from Miss Clarke's comforting arms to sidle closer to her brother. On the other hand, Miss Clarke appeared to be having difficulty in preserving her composure. By the indication of a persistent tug at the corners of her mouth, he wouldn't be surprised if Miss Clarke broke out in the giggles at any moment. "Please explain, my lord," she begged.

Julian bowed. "Certainly, Miss Clarke. My confusion is manifest by the odd notion I've conceived of wishing to meddle. Such behaviour is certainly uncharacteristic of me and, therefore, indicative of a confused mentality. My disordered speech is not presently apparent, perhaps, but will be when I ask Miss Tupper if she'd consider a position at Ashton House as a chambermaid."

He ignored Belle's delighted gasp of surprise and Jasper's grunt of disbelief, watching instead for Miss Clarke's reaction. She no longer presented a picture of suppressed merriment. He had astounded her, which astonishment clearly implied that she had not thought him capable of such a magnanimous gesture. *She* could be no more astounded than *he* was, however. But it was so satisfying to shock her, then watch her look of surprise soften to one of delight and gratitude.

"No, do not speak just yet," he forestalled her. "Let me finish. As for the hallucinations, they are represented by the nonsensical visions conjured up by supposing that Jasper would allow *me*—a total stranger and very likely a libertine like all the rest—to take his innocent sister to my home in distant Hampshire, which very likely is a positive den of iniquity."

Lily could not believe her ears. "What an *odd* man you are, my lord," she said, laughing. "You offer such a wonderful opportunity to this young woman, then you couch the offer in such horrid terms her poor brother cannot possibly know what to think or what to do!"

"Well, I know what to think *and* what to do!" Belle announced. "I will accept your offer without hesitation, because no one so kind as you, my lord, and married t'so kind a lady as *this,* could be a libertine!" She dried the last despiteful tear from her eye and vigorously blew her nose into Lord Ashton's handkerchief. Then, as if it were a triumphant gesture declaring the return of her courage and intention to meet life as an independent woman, she handed back the borrowed item.

Lord Ashton's lips quivered slightly as he gazed askance upon the deplorably wet and rumpled handkerchief. Once again, Lily was hard-pressed to maintain her composure. "Do keep the handkerchief, Miss Tupper," he said graciously. "I've a thousand of them. But I must tell you something. Firstly, Miss Clarke is not my wife. And secondly, the logic you used to bring yourself to the conclusion that I am *not* a libertine utterly escapes me. I could be trying to entrap you, foolish child!"

"Well, which't way is it?" exclaimed Jasper, exasperated by what he probably considered to be highflown roundaboutation. "*Are* you a libertine or *ain't* you? I wish't ye'd talk straight fer once't, milord!"

Jasper's honestly spoken words seemed to affect Lord Ashton quite strongly. The look of slightly smug humour fled from his face and a serious expression appeared. "Yes, Jasper, for once I shall 'talk straight.' Belle has nothing to fear from me. From whence the urge came to offer her a position in my house as a servant, I haven't the slightest idea. But I think she could be very happy there, well-fed, well recompensed for her duties, and amid kind people of high moral standards. In fact, she might find herself a bit stifled by all the doting attention she'd receive as soon as Mrs. Strand, my housekeeper, discovered that Belle is without a mother. Even were I inclined to seduce your sister, I should not be able to do so with so many eagle-eyed retainers at my house who have known me since I was in long clothes, and who used to box my ears whenever I was naughty!"

"And *I* can vouchsafe him, too," Lily offered spontaneously. "You see, if Lord Ashton were a libertine, he'd probably have tried to seduce *me* by now. He had every opportunity last night when we ate alone in the parlour at The Pig and Thistle."

Jasper and Belle looked slightly askance at these confessions, as though they hardly knew how to respond. Certainly they were confused about Lily's relationship to the viscount, and likely wondering how she happened to be travelling with him if she were not his wife.

At their ludicrous expressions, Lily choked on a little laugh and said, "I perceive that further explanations are in order. But it's so cold here, and I see that Bob and the other fellows have righted your carriage. And the wheel is as sound as ever it was before. Perhaps you had ought to meet us at the next inn and we can discuss Belle's future employment over a steamy dish of tea?" Then, belatedly remembering that Lord Ashton should be consulted on matters which directly affected him, such as the procurement of a new servant for his home in Hampshire, Lily enquired meekly, "Do you approve, Lord Ashton?"

A breeze caught the golden strands of hair that escaped from beneath the brim of his curly beaver hat and gently blew them across Lord Ashton's forehead. One tawny brow lifted in a mocking salute and his eyes brimmed with sly amusement. "And would it matter very much if I didn't?"

Lily thought about this for a moment, then answered, "You must know, my lord, I very much prefer having your approval than not! However, if you withhold your approval in this case I shall still try to convince you to see things my way. Papa says it is a fault of mine to be so stubborn!"

Lord Ashton laughed out loud, and the deep-timbred sound warmed Lily's blood. "Baggage!" he exclaimed with energy. "Get back to your patient, if you please!"

Lily started back to the carriage most willingly, for she knew now just exactly what he'd do. He turned to Jasper. "Do you agree to meet me at The Black Swan in Kempe's Corner, Mr. Tupper? It seems we are not destined to remain strangers, after all.''

Jasper, never much of a gabster, was made still more inarticulate by the unforeseen and rapidly moving events of the past half-hour. "Aye, milord."

"Very good, Mr. Tupper. Well, and what are all of *you* waiting for?" the viscount could be heard shouting with good-humoured alacrity at his gaping servants, all of whom were standing about in a seeming stupor. "Let's get this circus caravan on the road!"

Coachmen and grooms scrambled back onto their boxes, and the gig and both coaches resumed their journey towards their mutual assignation at The Black Swan.

BELLE'S FUTURE was decided over a nuncheon at The Black Swan that consisted of cold chicken, warm, crusty bread, red-currant jelly, sharp cheese and hot tea. Lord Ashton and Lily had supported Peter as he slowly walked inside to sit, eat, and finally to doze in front of the brisk fire that burnt in the parlour grate. Lord Ashton introduced him to the Tuppers first, of course, and the brother and sister were pleased to make the acquaintance of a young man who'd fought so admirably in the War. They were also relieved to understand that Lily was a vicar's daughter and travelling in Lord Ashton's entourage as Peter's nurse.

Pleshy and Janet ate with the other servants in the taproom, far away from Sebastian's nose-tickling fur. Sebastian seemed to have quickly developed a strong devotion to Peter, and had accompanied him inside the inn and was lying in the invalid's lap as he dozed by the fire. Sebastian's purring presence had a calming effect on Peter, which proved to be more conducive to sleep than the syrup of poppies, and without the drugging effects of the opiate. Though the more natural consequences of Sebastian's comfort could be found in the shed fur upon their clothes, no one seemed to mind except for Pleshy, whose task it was to brush his lordship's and Peter's coats, sneezing all the while.

Soon after nuncheon, Jasper trotted off to carry the bad tidings to Mr. Grampton that Belle would not be his bride, after all. He hoped the fellow would take the news well and not perhaps be tempted to bandy Belle's name about the village in a disrespectful manner. If he were so foolish as to do so, Jasper would certainly have to plant the fellow a facer. And, as he confided to Lord Ashton, he would not particularly relish sending to ground a decrepit old man who'd run to fat. It would not be sportsmanlike, no matter how necessary the action. Lord Ashton readily commiserated with him, and joined with Jasper in hoping that Mr. Grampton behaved himself.

When Jasper returned, he reported that though Mr. Grampton had ranted and raved at first, waving a large, sharp knife in one hand and a leg of mutton in the other, he had settled himself quickly enough and taken his disappointment in stride. And when Jasper explained how he would deal with the sort of sordid gossip that might be started by a jilted bridegroom, Mr. Grampton immediately agreed not to complain of any sort of ill-usage at the hands of his former fiancée.

Shortly thereafter, Jasper prepared to leave. He kissed Belle and muttered a tender, gruff goodbye, then promised Lord Ashton that he would visit Ashton House in a month's time to see how Belle got on, to make sure she was happy and being treated well, et cetera. Lord Ashton commended this plan and, from all that Jasper observed, his lordship did not betray a smidgen of the guilt which might be expected to be seen in the debauched expression of a libertine. And if he was not altogether sure about Lord Ashton, Jasper trusted Miss Clarke implicitly. Her innate goodness ensured that his sister would be both safe and well-treated. He felt certain that Belle had found a friend in the little vicar's daughter.

At the moment of departure, Belle stepped into the carriage with Pleshy and Janet, the one welcoming her with an abundance of French hospitality, the other looking sulky and displeased. As they rattled through town, they passed the butcher shop that was owned by Mr. Grampton. He stood outside on his front step as they trundled slowly past, a heavy scowl on his jowly face. Just as Belle had described him, he was round as a kettle, bald and wrinkled.

Lily was heartily sorry for Mr. Grampton and was tempted to request of Lord Ashton that they stop the carriage so that she might step down and speak a few comforting words, mixed, of course, with a strong reprimand for attempting to wed so young a girl as Belle. But when she looked at Lord Ashton, his expression made her almost suppose that he knew exactly what she was thinking and that he had no intention of pandering to another of her starts. Besides, after his kind and gracious offer to employ Belle and actually convey her to his estate in Hampshire, Lily dared not press her luck.

Lily picked at the little nubs of wool that had balled on her mittens and puzzled hard. What an enigma Lord Ashton was! What had made him behave so compassionately towards Belle? For as much as Lily had wanted to help the girl out of her dreadful situation, it had never occurred to her to suggest that Lord Ashton take so personal an interest in her. Did he regret his decision? By the grim look of him now, she thought he did.

"Don't cudgel your brain, my dear."

At the sound of Lord Ashton's low-spoken advice, Lily looked up. Peter was already asleep, and this must account for the viscount's whispering, but the slightly breathy tone of his deep voice made her arms erupt into gooseflesh. And the way he was looking at her didn't help a bit. The golden eyes were fixed on her in an intense, but tender gaze.

"What do you mean, my lord?"

"I mean I don't think you should try to understand why I did what I did today, or wonder if it heralds some transformation in my character, or if it means that I'm likely to do something of the same nature again. I don't even know myself.... But you can be sure of one thing—old habits are hard to break. I have been accustomed for some time now to mistrust and keep my distance from my fellow man. Don't expect too much of me. I fear you may only be disappointed.''

This little speech was delivered in a slightly sarcastic tone and with a small, self-derisive smile. Then Lord Ashton quite effectively removed the possibility of Lily pursuing further conversation by retreating behind his hat for another snooze, or at least the appearance of one.

Lily stared at Lord Ashton till a strong surge of longing flooding through her chest made her look away in confusion. She'd wanted to touch the viscount's firm lips and caress his lean jaw to remind herself that he was indeed flesh and blood and not a statue, as his cool-as-marble demeanour seemed to suggest.

But she knew he was far more than a statue, for she'd seen the warm spirit of humanity he strove to hide beneath his implacable and elegant exterior. And she could not help but expect a great deal from him, for she'd recognized the immense potential he possessed for doing good. She wanted with all her heart to help Lord Ashton embrace a philanthropic life. She anticipated with satisfaction how much the people around him would enjoy the benefits of his kindness. But a little voice inside her whispered something more—a poor, desperate voice that made the longing recur with a twist of pain. It said how wonderful, how truly wonderful it would be to share such a life with such a man.

CHAPTER SEVEN

DUSK STOLE OVER the Surrey countryside, casting the golden glow of sunset on the thatched roof of The Queen's Arms, a small, respectable inn situated in the south end of Cranbrook. After nuncheon at The Black Swan, Lord Ashton's "circus caravan" had not stopped again till Peter politely complained that he felt absolutely pulled to pieces from bumping about in the carriage all day. Lord Ashton immediately ordered his horsemen to stop at the next town and its first decent inn.

Lily had just returned from Peter's room, where she had cajoled him into eating a very small dinner. His appetite was all but gone, he was flushed and a little warm, and he seemed much more tired today than he'd been the previous afternoon. She was worried about him, but knew that his symptoms were probably just the accumulated effects of sheer exhaustion. She herself was in perfect health, yet still felt the bruising shock of an extended journey over weatherbeaten roads. She hoped a good night's rest would restore Peter to greater stamina for the last leg of their trip on the morrow.

Janet, obviously in a bit of a pet, sat on the edge of Lily's bed, swinging her wooden leg back and forth like a restless child in Sunday school. Lily sat beside her on the quilted counterpane that covered the narrow bed. She stroked the long braid of blond hair that fell down Janet's back. "What's the matter, Janet?" she asked her.

"Oh, nothin', miss," Janet replied evasively. "I'm just tired, I expect."

"I see." Lily waited for a moment, then enquired, "Do your blue-devils have anything to do with our new travelling companion?"

Janet's gaze met Lily's, then self-consciously slid away. "I don't know what ye mean, miss."

"I think you do. And it's perfectly understandable that you might be a little jealous of her. She's quite pretty."

"So you think she's pretty, too," Janet muttered dejectedly.

"But no more so than you," Lily returned.

Janet stopped her peg-leg mid-swing and held it elevated for Lily's inspection. She flicked her hand in a disparaging gesture. "But *this* ain't too fetchin'. And not even you, miss, kin make me believe it is."

"Your wooden leg won't matter a fig to a worthy man, Janet," Lily said gently. "While we are attracted to people physically, or repulsed, like Belle was by poor Mr. Grampton, there's certainly more to falling in love than a person's physical appearance. I daresay Belle might have liked Mr. Grampton if she'd had the opportunity to get to know him, and if he'd been a good, kind man, which, I'm afraid, seems doubtful in this case! But it's what qualities lie inside a person which truly make you like or dislike him or her. You've so much that's good in you, Janet!"

Janet lowered her leg to the floor, her face brightening a little. "Pleshy don't seem t'mind m'leg. We talk and laugh and I never catch 'im starin' at it, like some folk do. He even asked me to tell 'im how it happened, and ye know I'd much rather a person was straightforward in askin' me about it than to shy away like it was too shameful t'speak of!"

Lily was surprised and impressed by Pleshy's tactful handling of the subject. "That was well done of Pleshy. And I'm sure he likes you, my dear. Your good humour makes you decidedly easy to be around, you know."

Janet glowed. But now was the difficult part. Lily must put Janet on her guard without setting up her hackles and pushing the girl to do the exact opposite of what she ought to do to protect herself. Lily took Janet's hand and held it affectionately. "But I don't suppose you have heard that Pleshy is reputed to be rather, er, addicted to liking a great many women. Lord Ashton tells me that Pleshy is a flirt and not likely to settle on just one woman, no matter how much he admires her."

Janet opened her mouth to speak, but Lily rushed on, "You mustn't think I blame you! I daresay Pleshy has very engaging manners, but it would be remiss of me if I did not put a little flea in your ear. I don't wish you to break your heart, Janet!''

Janet's blue eyes widened. ''Oh, miss, I'm not so stupid as that! I know Pleshy's a flirt. He tol' me himself, and even said that Lord Ashton threatened 'im with losin' 'is job if he so much as clapped a finger on me!''

''He did?''

''Yes, miss. But Pleshy told me that his lordship said it in a friendly way, 'cause he knew Pleshy'd do what he was bid t'do without havin' t'threaten 'im with dismissal. He's been 'is lordship's valet fer five years, miss, and they's as close t'bein' friends as any servant and 'is master.''

''Well, I'm glad that Lord Ashton has such estimable influence over his servants. And I'm equally glad that you're going to be sensible about Pleshy.''

Janet's nose wrinkled. ''I never said as how I'd be *sensible,* miss! I can't help it! I like him considerable. He's kind, and he tells such good stories, all about his French mum and his Scots dad and all 'is brothers and sisters. And he's so handsome, miss, sometimes I kin hardly breathe from lookin' at 'im!''

Lily could well imagine how avidly Janet would listen to amusing and heart-warming stories about a large family, since she had been orphaned and had endured such a deplorable childhood before coming to the vicarage. Pleshy certainly knew what would entertain the girl, and he seemed to be taking pains to do so. But Janet's blunt confession that she could not guarantee to be sensible was worrisome to Lily. She hoped she could depend entirely upon Lord Ashton's confidence in his manservant to clap not even a finger on Janet. The girl's besotted condition made her very vulnerable.

"Janet, you were raised in a foundling home. You know what it's like to be without parents. Even denied one parent, a child is at a disadvantage—"

Janet looked horrified. "Oh, miss! Ye mustn't think I meant that I wouldn't be sensible about *that!* I'm not about to share my warmin' pan with Pleshy! What I meant was, I can't help it if'n I fall in love with 'im! But—Lor', miss!—I would never do *that!*"

Lily breathed a sigh of relief, and now felt a bit embarrassed about leaping to conclusions. "I'm glad to hear that, my dear. I didn't think you would. I was just afraid... Put in tempting circumstances, you know—"

Janet cut her off, saying with a laugh, "Don't worry, miss. I didn't take it amiss, what ye said. I understand ye're jest lookin' out fer me, as ye always do and have done since yer pa took me away from that wretched home!" Seriously, she added, "I'd never do anythin' that would make ye ashamed of me. Yer pa taught me better'n that!"

"It relieves me to hear you speak so," Lily said warmly. "But, while you've quite put me at ease about your virtue, I'm still worried about your heart, my dear!"

Janet sighed and looked a little woeful. "So am I, miss. But there's nothin' I kin do about it. I jest want t'enjoy what's left of my time with Pleshy. If'n my heart's broke when we go back t'th' vicarage, I expect I'll learn to get by."

"It's all my doing, you know!" Lily said, standing up abruptly and pacing the floor in front of the fireplace. "I probably should have brought Cathy along as chaperon, not you! But I thought you might enjoy... However, I should have known! You're just a child yourself, and I—"

"Lord, miss, it's half past six!" exclaimed Janet, breaking into Lily's self-condemnatory monologue. "Lord Ashton said ye was to join 'im in the parlour at seven and ye're not even dressed yet. Come, let's get you started, miss!"

Though she was not done with feeling absolutely riddled with remorse from having put Janet in the way of having her heart broken, Lily allowed the girl to coax her into the chair in front of a small dressing-table which, due to an uneven leg, leaned a little to one side. She stared into the slightly warped mirror and was alarmed to see how disheveled she looked. She might be wretched and penitent, but she would not sit at table with the impeccable Lord Ashton in such a state of disarray.

"Brush my hair till my scalp tingles, Janet. I feel like a hag!"

"I will. I'll brush it till the copper shines out'it, miss!"

This reminder of the copper, or russet, highlights in her hair also reminded Lily of something else. "You're to join me in the parlour, Janet. I know you're probably tired, and I'm very sorry to keep you from your bed. But Lord Ashton insisted that you play chaperon tonight."

"I know, miss. He told me hisself," Janet informed her while she plied her brush with energy. "I've not been the chaperon I should be, miss, but tonight I'll sit in the parlour with ye as long as needs be, and with my eyes never strayin' from looking at the two of ye!"

The amusing picture this well-intended threat conjured up made Lily smile. "I feel much safer now."

Janet must have caught the lack of seriousness in Lily's tone and fixed her mistress with a sapient eye. "Don't think he don't like ye, miss, or that ye don't need a chaperon, 'cause 'less I'm losin' my sense, his lordship likes ye considerable."

Lily watched in the mirror as her smile slid from her face. She didn't trust herself to reply to Janet's pronouncement. And she didn't at all like the pleasurable sensation that fluttered like butterflies through her at Janet's expressed opinion that Lord Ashton "liked her considerable." It would not be sensible at all to be flattered by such a nobleman's fleeting admiration, if, indeed, there truly was admiration there. In a few days, this entire journey and all its diverse travellers would be consigned permanently to the past. Lily must follow her own advice to Janet and be "sensible." After all, she had no desire to imitate her abigail's headlong—albeit unwilling—rush towards a broken heart.

"MY LORD, I DO HOPE you mean to take the *animal* downstairs with you. If you do not, I'm sure its yowling will eventually awaken the captain."

Perceiving a slight suggestion of dullness in the mirror-like surface of his freshly polished boots, Julian rubbed the toe of his Hessian against the back of his leg. "I will, Pleshy," he said as another of Sebastian's irritated *meows* from the hallway penetrated the thick door of the chamber. "It seems I have no choice. Besides waking Peter, he would very likely annoy the other patrons of the inn as well. I hope he does not object to accompanying me to the parlour. I do not fancy my new jacket marred by claw marks."

Pleshy's lips twitched and he brushed the shoulder of Julian's Bishop's blue jacket with an open palm, his sharp eyes scouring the superfine for even the tiniest piece of lint. "Per'aps if you feed 'im, my lord, he'll go willingly enough. But I know he won't shut 'is trap all night unless he's allowed to sleep with the captain. He grew attached to 'im uncommon fast."

"That he did," agreed Julian. "But Peter had been attracting cats at the vicarage, too. I would not cater to this particular feline's demands, however, except that I have the lowering suspicion that he has a beneficial effect on Peter. Helps him relax, it seems."

"At least the drat creature has one redeemable quality," said Pleshy. "I only wish't he weren't so full of fur!"

Lord Ashton picked a long yellow hair from his lapel and murmured, "Don't we all. How *did* you miss this one, Pleshy? I don't expect that dinner will be of a long duration tonight. And as soon as we've dined, I'll bring Miss Clarke up to check on Peter." Julian looked worriedly at Peter's flushed face as he turned restlessly on his pillow. "He's not quite the thing tonight, is he? What's your opinion, Pleshy?"

"I think Miss Clarke's got the right of it in thinking that the captain's just done up, so t'speak. I only hope his fever don't climb too high."

"If necessary, we can stay on at the inn another day so that he can rest. And there's bound to be some sort of doctor or apothecary nearby, should Peter's condition require a second opinion."

"Miss Clarke'd be miffed if you brought in some strange doctor, my lord."

Julian smiled. "Yes, she would, wouldn't she? Well, she needn't worry, for I'm more willing to trust Peter entirely into Miss Clarke's care than to some provincial quack. With luck, our patient will be much better on the morrow and we can proceed. We're so close to being home."

Pleshy looked thoughtful. "It'll be odd sayin' goodbye to them, won't it? Janet's a taking little thing, wooden leg'n all."

Julian darted a keen look at his valet. "Waxing sentimental, Pleshy? You *are* minding my admonition, aren't you?"

Pleshy lifted his chin. "Of course I am, my lord! And you didn't need to tell me to, neither. I never intended to befoul the chit. She's too sweet and innocent for that sort of slap and tickle."

"Good God, the little Clarke's saintly spirit has inspired even my rakish valet to dust off his conscience! And about time, I'd say," Julian said, laughing.

Pleshy grinned. "No tellin' how long it'll last, my lord. Not long, I hope. Just till Janet's on her way home, I expect."

"Then it's Janet's influence and not Miss Clarke's that has brought you to this pass, my friend," Julian warned him playfully. "Watch yourself, Pleshy, or it's parson's mousetrap for you!"

Pleshy shrugged and looked sheepish. Julian enjoyed another laugh at the expense of his valet, then exited the chamber, wondering at the effect Janet's ingenuous love of life had wrought on Pleshy's jaded heart. As he closed the door behind him, Sebastian rose up on his back legs and placed his front paws on Julian's knee. He yowled soulfully.

"Yes, I pity you," Julian said, dropping his hand to Sebastian's head for a brief caress. "But you cannot see him till after I've eaten my dinner. In the meantime, you must endure the company of less beloved beings like myself and Miss Clarke. Come along." Then he lifted Sebastian into his arms, imag-

ining with patient resignation the fur that would cling
to his new jacket as a result.

LILY SAT ON A SMALL SOFA with Janet, waiting for
Lord Ashton to enter the parlour. She slid a slightly
tremulous hand up the back of her neck to collect stray
wisps of hair and to endeavour to tuck them into the
knot that Janet had arranged at the nape. The maid
had brushed Lily's hair till it shone as glossy as silk,
but that was the limit to her talent as a *coiffeuse*. As
always one strand of chestnut hair fell forward on
Lily's cheek, and tonight, due to Janet's well-meaning
but fumbled execution, several strands also fell down
her neck. Oh, well. Lord Ashton knew Janet was not
adept as an abigail. Lily's haphazard hairstyle would
simply attest to that.

And as for chaperoning, Janet obviously did not
perceive it as very exciting or as much of a challenge,
because already she was growing drowsy. She had
brought some handwork to do, and she was nodding
over her stitchery like a drooping flower full of evening dew.

When the door opened and Lord Ashton entered
with Sebastian in his arms, Janet did not even look up.
But how anyone could doze while the room was elec-
trified with the viscount's vital presence was a huge
mystery to Lily. She felt the man's daunting energy
invade her every nerve, a feeling not unlike what she
imagined the moon's powerful effect to be on the ebb
and flow of tides—mystical, compelling, irresistible.

Goodness, she had become poetic in her thinking, hadn't she? What would Papa say?

But looking at Lord Ashton in his deep blue jacket and black pantaloons, glossy boots and snowy neck-cloth, she did not wonder at her sudden digression into a poet's metaphorical inclination. However, it was the man inside the clothes that inspired her, rather than the clothes themselves. The superb elegance of the tailoring only served as a becoming setting for his ex-quisite manly beauty. Lily blushed at the continued poetical nature of her shockingly wayward thoughts.

Could Lord Ashton possibly be aware of how flat-tering a picture he and the majestic Sebastian pre-sented? If he had been a tulip of the ton intent on making a great impression upon first entering an ex-alted drawing-room, he could not have chosen a com-panion that would have had more effect on the sensibilities of the inhabitants of said drawing-room. The cat, with its regal bearing and aloof demeanour, was a perfect complement to Lord Ashton's particu-lar kind of beauty. And they matched. Perfectly. Yel-low hair, golden eyes, large, graceful figures. But they were related, were they not? Each was either a de-scendent of or compared to the King of Beasts.

"You do not speak, Miss Clarke," Lord Ashton said in a low voice. "Are you wishful of not waking your chaperon?"

Lily might have imagined it, but she had the dis-tinct impression that while she had been openly star-ing at Lord Ashton, he had been returning her perusal with equal interest. She trembled at such an idea. Certainly he could not be admiring *her* as she had been admiring him! She self-consciously smoothed the skirts of her sprigged gown. In the same travel-creased dress of the night before and with her hair all in a tumble, she could hardly hope to inspire admiration even remotely similar to that which he inspired in her.

She ducked her head. "No, my lord. I don't mind if you rouse her, but I still do not see the need for a chaperon," she finished, a hint of dejection creeping into her voice despite her earnest endeavour to sound unaffected.

She felt rather than heard him approach her. His footsteps were hushed by the carpet. She felt the tip of his finger under her chin. He pressed gently and tilted her face so that their eyes met. "You are a fool, Miss Clarke, if you do not perceive the need for a chaperon," he said in a whisper, his voice seducing all her senses at once. "Either that, or you're the most modest young woman I've ever encountered. But I can assure you of this—tonight you most definitely require a chaperon."

He removed the intoxicating pressure of his finger and turned to Janet. "Wake up, Janet," he said in a slightly raised voice. Janet's head jerked up and her hands splayed over her open workbox. When she saw Lord Ashton, she sat up as straight as a maypole.

"Goodness, miss!" she said, her eyelids fluttering in an attempt to recover a measure of wakefulness. "How *ever* did I nod off like that? I assure you, miss—my Lord Ashton—I will *not* fall asleep again. See, I'm as watchful as a hungry buzzard!''

Janet demonstrated her good intentions by assuming a pose not entirely dissimilar to the morbid posturing of the scavenger she had compared herself to. Lily nearly laughed, and welcomed the inclination towards merriment as a diversion with which to break the spell Lord Ashton's closeness had weaved upon her. She must be ''sensible,'' she told herself firmly.

''I'm famished, my lord,'' she lied, standing up and moving quickly to the table. ''And I don't think I ought to linger over my dinner tonight. I'm anxious to look in on Peter.''

Lord Ashton set down Sebastian and followed her to the table. His fluid, graceful movements were most disconcerting. ''And I'm just as anxious that you do.'' He reached for the bell-pull that hung by the rough mantelshelf over the rustic fireplace. ''We'll eat immediately.''

Dinner was served promptly and Lily forced down as much food as she could. They ate pretty much in silence, with only an occasional comment on the most commonplace subjects. Sebastian paced back and forth in front of the door which led into the hall, now and then letting loose a mournful ''meow.'' Lily had fed him a few morsels from the table when they'd first sat down, but once his appetite had been satisfied he could not be tempted away from his vigil at the door.

The beneficial effects of the food on her depleted energy also helped calm Lily's nerves, and she was able after a while to compose herself sufficiently to look shyly up from her plate at the viscount. She encountered a warm gaze that nearly made her return to the contemplation of her raisin pie. But she steeled herself and said, by way of light conversation, "I see Sebastian is as devoted as we feared he'd be."

Lord Ashton grinned ruefully and did not reply.

"I'm curious," Lily continued, smiling. "How have you managed to bed down all of the various members of your circus caravan?"

Lord Ashton lifted his table napkin and dabbed at his mouth before speaking. "It was not easy, Miss Clarke," he confessed. "Belle is sharing quarters with one of the inn's chambermaids, the coachmen are berthed as usual with the stable-lads, and Pleshy does indeed boast possession of his very own chamber. No! Don't apologize—I don't mind. We were fortunate that the proprietor had another room, because there are other patrons and the inn is not very large. As you may well imagine, the undertaking of such a task as this has made me feel rather like the headmaster of a board-school, or like the old woman who lived in a shoe, perhaps."

Lily laughed. "'She had so many children, she didn't know what to do!' A comparison I would never have conceived in a million years! Rather you should be called '*Father* Goose!'"

"So, you don't think all this nurturing I'm doing has unmanned me, eh?"

His voice was teasing, but his eyes held a serious expression. She replied in kind. "Hardly, my lord. As I told Peter, a man's mettle is not measured entirely by his physical strength or the other masculine attributes we admire in the male sex, rather he is shown to be most manly when he is not afraid to demonstrate his tender side, as well."

Lord Ashton had no reply to this, but his look was eloquent. Lily could hardly credit it, but Lord Ashton seemed most interested in her opinion on this matter and appeared pleased with what she'd said. Could it be that their philosophies were not so opposite as she'd supposed?

They smiled at each other over the table for some time, till the sound of a soft thud recalled them to their surroundings. They looked towards the sofa and observed that Janet had fallen onto her side, her head resting on the sofa arm, and she was softly snoring.

"She had been weaving to and fro for some time," Lily commented with a chuckle.

"But she might have stayed awake a *little* longer. It seems we were not alarming her enough by our behaviour to keep her sufficiently interested. How ironic that she should fall fast asleep just when her chaperonage was most needed!"

Lily turned abruptly to look at Lord Ashton. What could he mean? He rose from the table and moved to stand in front of her. He had the oddest, most compelling expression in his eyes. He reached for her hand and she gave it him, mindlessly. He pulled her to her feet and against his chest, where she nestled quite agreeably. He lifted her chin with his forefinger, just as he'd done earlier. Her eyes met his, his head bent to hers. Their lips were nearly touching.

"My lord?" It was Pleshy's voice that intruded into Lily's misty state of pleasurable confusion. "Oh—Good God—you must excuse me! *Achoo!*"

Lily wasn't sure whether she pulled away or was gently pushed away. All she knew was that she had one moment been in Lord Ashton's arms and on the point of being kissed, and in the next, she was standing alone and feeling bereft. But as the yearning to be back in his arms was viciously suppressed, a feeling of embarrassment stole over her. She had been foolish, and Pleshy had witnessed her folly. Not that he was making her uncomfortable by staring at her, for he was too busy sneezing.

"What is it, Pleshy?" Lord Ashton asked his valet in a rather hoarse voice. "I should hope it's something important to have left Peter alone!"

"It is, my lord. *Achoo!* It's Peter, my lord. *A-achoo!* He's so restless. He's asking for Miss Clarke. I said I would fetch her. He's doing poorly, my lord. Has a fever. Oh, drat this nose! *A-a-achoo!*"

"I will go to him immediately," said Lily, slipping past Pleshy and into the hall. Sebastian had already darted between Pleshy's legs and was quickly ascending the stairs to the upper floor. Lily was concerned about Peter, but she was also glad to be able to remove herself from Lord Ashton's presence long enough for her blush to subside and her heart to resume its normal rhythm. No doubt she would lie awake half the night chastising herself for behaving so stupidly, but for now she would try to forget that she'd allowed herself to be so easily pulled into the viscount's arms. While it troubled her that Lord Ashton would trifle with her in such a manner, her response was what alarmed her the most. What would Papa say if he knew she'd behaved like a positive *lightskirt?*

When Lily reached Peter's chamber, Lord Ashton had caught her up, having bounded up the stairs two at a time. They entered the room together and discovered Peter trying to get out of bed. He had pushed himself to a sitting position and had thrown one emaciated leg over the edge. He looked dazed and unsteady. Lily and Lord Ashton both hurried over to the bed, standing one on each side, and gently urged him to lie down again.

Peter grasped Lily's hand, and she was alarmed to find his palm so hot and dry. "Lily...? Where've you been? I'm thirsty!"

Lily straightened his blankets and pulled them up to just below Peter's chin. His lips were parched and his sunken cheeks glowed with high colour. "Stay still a moment, Peter, and I'll pour you a glass of cool water. There, there, now. Don't squirm so!"

But Peter *would* squirm. "Can't get comfortable, Lily. Feel as though I'm still lurching along on that dreadful road! All my bones ache. Julian?"

Lord Ashton leaned over the bed while Lily poured a glass of water from a crock which had been placed on the table next to the bed. "What is it, Peter?"

Peter smiled wanly at his uncle. "Feel like the veriest fribble, lying here! Got the headache, you know. Seems like there's a herd of cows running from ear to ear!"

"You're understandably exhausted, Nephew," Lord Ashton soothed him. "You'll feel better tomorrow."

"My lord, please support Peter while I help him take a sip of this water," said Lily. "Not too much at once, Peter," she cautioned as he gulped greedily from the glass. "You can have more in a few minutes." Lord Ashton lowered him back into his pillow.

"Just like Pleshy," Peter complained teasingly. "You won't let me drink a whole glass at once. He says I'd likely cast up my accounts if I drank too much too fast."

"He's right," Lily assured him. "And now the best thing for you to do is sleep." She reached for Peter's hand and put two fingers on his wrist to check his pulse.

Peter turned his hand and grasped Lily's. He looked up at her pleadingly. "Stay for a while. I feel better when you're nearby."

"Sebastian's not enough?" she quizzed him, smiling. The cat had nestled against Peter's thigh and was already purring.

Peter chuckled weakly and reached down to stroke Sebastian's fur. "He's well enough, but I'd still like *you* to stay, Lily." Peter's eyes drifted shut, his forehead creasing in an expression of pain. "You and Julian, of course," he said, his voice fast fading.

"Lie very still, Peter, so you don't disturb Sebastian," Lily whispered, hoping the idea of pandering to the cat's comfort would encourage him to be less restless.

His eyes opened fractionally, then closed. "Still as can be, Lily," he promised.

Judging by his even breathing, Peter seemed to have fallen rather abruptly to sleep. Lily looked across the bed at Lord Ashton. Their gazes met in mutual worry. "I won't go to bed," she said. "He'll have need of me, I'm sure. His fever is high. He'll probably sleep for a few minutes, then awaken again. You don't mind if I—I mean, you can't really go to bed with *me* in here, can you? Ah, but there's Pleshy's room, isn't there?"

"You don't seriously imagine that I would go to bed in Pleshy's room, leaving you alone to stand watch over Peter all night, do you?" He gestured towards the truckle-bed that stood against the opposite wall. "When you get tired, you can lie down there and nap while I sit with Peter. We'll take turns."

Lily felt her former embarrassment return. She remembered how he'd nearly kissed her, and would certainly have done so had Pleshy not interrupted them. And she remembered, too, that she would have *let* him kiss her. Now she was destined to spend the entire night in the same room with him. Though Peter would be present, he would be asleep or confused most of the time. But under such circumstances, surely Lord Ashton would not attempt to kiss her again!

"I don't expect I shall be able to rest at all, Lord Ashton," she said quite truthfully, fussily smoothing Peter's pillow casing. "It's hard enough to try to sleep in a strange bed, but when you are worried about someone—"

"About whom are you worried, Miss Clarke?" Lord Ashton asked her quietly.

Startled, Lily looked up. Lord Ashton's expression was enigmatic. His golden eyes glowed lustrously in the candlelight from the three-tapered brace on the table next to the bed. The slight slant of his mouth lent him an air of tender amusement.

Lily blushed and answered, "Why, I was speaking of my concern for Peter, of course. I wasn't—"

"You weren't speaking of me, then? I should think you'd be worried about whether or not I'd try to kiss you again," he said wryly. "And I can't say that I blame you. Do you want me to fetch Janet? But she would only go to sleep herself! And Pleshy would keep Peter awake with his sneezing."

Lily dropped her head and mumbled, "I'm sure you would not take advantage of a situation like this. Peter is ill, and—and you're as worried as I am."

Lily heard him sigh. "You're right," he agreed, but there was a definite ring of resignation in his voice that half thrilled, half terrified Lily. "I am not such a scoundrel as to try to kiss you under these circumstances. In fact, Miss Clarke, I promise not to take advantage of any further opportunities which might come my way. I owe you an apology. Will you forgive me for succumbing to that dratted sobriquet I am encumbered with?''

Lily lifted her head. "You mean 'The Lion'?"

He smiled. "No, my dear. 'Man of the world, seducer of women.'''

His smile was so engaging, so infectious, and his apology seemed so sincere. Lily could not help herself, her smile dimpled in response. "As you know, my lord, I am generally most forgiving. That is what Papa taught us. It says in the scriptures that one must forgive seventy times seven.''

Lord Ashton's eyebrows lifted wickedly. "Ah, then I can misbehave at least four-hundred-and-eighty-nine times more, and still be forgiven?''

Lily laughed, albeit rather nervously. In more than one respect, it was going to be a long night.

CHAPTER EIGHT

JULIAN HAD POSITIONED a chair for Miss Clarke next to the bed, where she could easily keep watch of Peter. He got another for himself and placed it on the opposite side where he had a good view of Peter and a good view of Miss Clarke, as well—a visual feast of pain and pleasure. It was painful to see Peter suffer, yet it was so gratifying to watch his pretty nurse show by example that her inner compassion was as attractive as her outer appearance.

As Miss Clarke had predicted, Peter slept for about twenty minutes, then awoke very hot and restless. She applied a cool, wet cloth to his forehead and gave him a drink, Julian assisting as before. Then she soothed and reassured him in that melodic voice of hers till Peter once again fell asleep. During these procedures, Sebastian removed himself from trouble's way to the very farthest end of the bed and watched solemnly. As soon as Peter settled down, he returned to his former position against Peter's thigh.

"It seems rather uncanny," opined Julian, when they had both resumed their stations, "but that cat seems to understand what's going on."

"They are perceptive creatures," Miss Clarke commented, tucking back that ever-present strand of loose hair. She smiled, but with an effort. She looked tired and pale. Julian felt a pang of shame, knowing that part of what she'd had to endure that evening had been his fault. He should never have given in to that overwhelming urge to kiss her. And in the end he had the remorse, but no memory of a kiss to make it worthwhile. Pleshy's interruption had taken care of that. Certainly it would be wrong to dally with the virtuous little Clarke, but her response to him when he held her was so...intriguing. But with each consecutive hour he spent in Miss Clarke's company, she became more and more intriguing, and in more and more ways.

"Why do you carry a pistol in your greatcoat pocket, Lord Ashton?"

Lost in his own tantalizing and speculative thoughts, Julian was surprised by the question. "What makes you think I carry a weapon on my person, Miss Clarke?" he returned, feeling suddenly on the defence. He knew she wouldn't approve.

She shrugged her shoulders. "It was a simple deduction to make. I saw you reach inside your pocket when we stopped to help the Tuppers. You were holding on to something. I did not suppose it was a good-luck charm. Cynics do not believe in such nonsense." She smiled teasingly. Whether she approved of him or not, she did not appear to be of a mind to pass judgement upon him.

He relaxed a little, then tensed again as he considered whether or not to tell her the truth. It would be easy enough to say that he had taken up the habit because of an excess of highwaymen on the roads lately, et cetera. But that was only partially true. He had been carrying the weapon for years, ever since Richard was killed. He observed the patient, yet intensely interested, expression in her brown eyes. Suddenly it seemed completely fitting that she should know the truth, that she had a right, somehow, to expect total honesty from him.

"You do not have to tell me if you'd rather not," she demurred kindly, shifting her eyes away and allowing him the time and privacy he needed to make up his mind. It seemed Miss Clarke's perception rivalled that of the cat's. Somehow she knew that there was a particular reason behind Julian's decision to arm himself.

"Has Peter told you that I'm the youngest of three sons, Miss Clarke?" Julian began abruptly.

She looked up. "Yes. He said your two older brothers had died. That's all."

Julian's lips curled bitterly. "Yes, 'that's all!' Dead and buried and forgotten by most. And so it is in the common way of things. People die and life goes on. But for me it has not been so easy to forget."

"We don't forget them, my lord. But we do have to let them go, in a sense, in order to continue living our own lives," Miss Clarke said earnestly, the sympathy in her voice and expression nearly breaking through the wall of protection he had constructed so long ago.

Julian hardened his heart against her assault. "That is a platitude, Miss Clarke, and one that I've heard a hundred times if I've heard it once."

She flinched, and he was sorry he'd hurt her. "I don't mean to be rude," he said in an altered tone. "But I find the use of hackneyed phrases as a means to reason and explain away grief a sadly useless endeavour."

"That is because the language we use to express our feelings is inadequate, my lord," Miss Clarke persisted. "You must look beyond the platitudes and into the hearts of the people who are trying to help you. It is hard to find an original way to express grief or encouragement. We are simply at a loss for words."

Julian heaved a sigh and shook his head. "Richard was murdered, Miss Clarke," he revealed bluntly, expecting her to look shocked, to murmur something incoherent and to drop the subject altogether. After all, murder was such a distasteful topic, especially to gently reared ladies. But she did not respond in the manner he expected.

"How?" she asked, her sweet face grave and expressing sorrow, but hardly hysterical and certainly not displaying aversion to the subject.

"Now you will understand my lack of sympathy towards the generality of thieves," he prefaced his story, then began, "Richard was, as you would be very pleased to know, a confirmed philanthropist, Miss

Clarke. He had the kindest heart in all of London, I'd wager. He was forever helping out the indigent and deprived. He was as sorry as you are for the circumstances beyond their control which he was sure had thrust most criminals into a life of felony.''

"You must have loved him very much," she interjected softly.

Julian repressed the surge of pain and snapped, "I loved him, but he was a fool! He was strolling home from a rout one clear spring night. Richard was positively idiotish for the beauties of nature, and half the time had his head in the clouds. This night he was most probably lost in the stars and wasn't paying attention to where he was wandering. He ended up in a quarter rather rougher than he was used to and was approached by a beggar. Mind you, the man didn't demand Richard's blunt or anything of the sort. He merely begged Richard for a small pittance to help buy himself and his family a bit of food."

"And I suppose he gave it to him?" Miss Clarke prompted when Julian paused to compose himself.

"Of course he did!" Julian replied. "Richard was an easy touch to anyone who came in his way. He did not think it right that he should have so much, and many other people so little. He gave the beggar a generous donation, but when the scurvy fellow saw Richard's purse—which Richard, in his naïvety, had not even thought to conceal or protect—the man's greed got the better of him. He pulled a knife and stabbed Richard, then ran off with the purse."

She made a little gasping noise. A moment of silence passed, then she asked, "How do you come by this story? Your brother must have remained conscious long enough to tell someone what had happened to him."

"Yes. Richard refused to allow his coach to drive behind him when he strolled, as many people do in the case that they might get tired or meet up with some ruffians. But Richard's coachman thought his master a bit too trusting and he did follow behind, but at such a distance Richard never knew about it. In this situation, his coach and servants came upon him just after the beggar ran off. Richard told them what had happened before he died."

"How very dreadful for you."

"And how very dreadful for Richard's fiancée. He was to be married that spring."

A pall fell over the room, a natural result of such a sad story. Miss Clarke was sincerely sorry—you could see the sympathy plainly writ on her face. But she was not daunted or plunged into despair. His experience with her so far had made him of the opinion that Miss Clarke was not afraid to face things and deal with them straight on. Her next words were in character with this observation.

"You believe your brother's naïvety and trustfulness, his compassion towards unfortunate people—whether of a criminal character or not—killed him."

"Yes. And I challenge you to dispute me."

"I can't. You're quite right."

Julian had expected an argument, or at least an attempt to explain away what had happened to Richard without deprecating his brother's philanthropic ways. He could not help but voice his amazement. "I'm surprised you do not try to convince me otherwise!"

"Not even for the sake of encouraging you to be more trustful and compassionate yourself would I take up an argument I cannot support! But you will forgive me, I hope, if I do say *one* thing!"

"I thought you must have at least one thing to say," murmured Julian, a tiny smile tugging at the corners of his lips.

"One can be a philanthropist without putting one's self in harm's way, as your brother did. I suspect he was not a very sensible man, and he probably did not keep his wits about him as he ought. I believe in allowing people the benefit of the doubt, but need and want are such strong urges amongst the poor, I don't think I should have tempted the beggar by allowing him to see my purse, nor would I have walked alone in an unsafe quarter. In short, your brother's philanthropic ways definitely contributed to the circumstances of his death, but his carelessness made it all but inevitable. And lastly, I do not know why you base your opinion of people so much on this one incident. Surely the good people you've met must outnumber the bad!"

"Surely the damage bad people do outweigh the benevolence done by good people, no matter how many there may be!" countered Lord Ashton.

"Only if you allow it to be so! Looking back to our initial argument at the vicarage, I believe our principles make all the difference in how we see the world! I, for one, choose to see it as a good place. And when one has that sort of view, and tries to make his own small contribution by doing good, things are certainly more apt to improve than if he sits about bitterly lamenting all the wrongs and injustices. One is so much more stimulating than the other, and so much better a way to live our lives, don't you think?"

Towards the end of Miss Clarke's condensed sermon—for Julian could not perceive it as anything but—she had begun to look a trifle anxious and to speak a little more quickly. No doubt she thought she might have gone too far and had offended him. Julian admitted to himself that had the sermon been delivered by a sanctimonious old rector with a wart on his nose, he'd not have withstood the barely disguised assault on his sybaritic style of life and care-for-nobody ways. But when Miss Clarke spoke, one knew with a certainty that she was completely sincere and well intended, believing with a fervour everything that tumbled out of her pretty, bow-shaped mouth.

Julian was enchanted, but he still did not believe her philosophy could possibly withstand the test of time. She had not lived on this wicked earth for very long.

"I know what you're thinking and I disagree!" Miss Clarke told him. "I don't believe I'll change my views on these matters! But never mind that! I don't wish to argue with you. However, I do wish you will tell me about your other brother. Or would you rather not?''

"Tom was in the army. He died at Oporto, in Portugal, just a few months after Richard was killed. The worst of it was he was not even shot by the enemy, but was erroneously felled by a fellow officer. He was on his way home, but died of an infection to the wound before he reached the coast.''

"That must have been a horrible blow to endure so soon after Richard's death! I do not wonder that you became disillusioned!''

Julian snorted. "I was more than disillusioned, Miss Clarke. I was bitterly disappointed and unhappy. I abandoned all my former lofty ambitions—though that was a moot point, since I was forced of necessity to set aside the plans I'd made before I inherited the title—and I embraced all of the profligate habits and dissipated activities I had used to think were a waste of time.''

"What *were* your ambitions before you inherited the title, my lord?''

Julian gave a bark of unamused laughter. "Ha! You will be astonished! I was destined for the Church, Miss Clarke. I—the frippery fellow you see before you to-day—was to be the vicar of Pleasely!''

But Miss Clarke did not display astonishment, nor did she laugh. Rather he had never seen her appear so sober. His own forced merriment faltered and, as the object of her serious scrutiny, he became most uncomfortable.

"On the contrary, I am not astonished. Rather I think I understand you better. To be *so* disillusioned as you are now, you must have been at some time as full of hope as me."

"Worse than you," Julian admitted, shuddering. "Too hopeful, too trusting, too well intended. Undoubtedly I set myself in the way of disappointment."

"You would have been a wonderful vicar, I make no doubt," she said at last, her eyes narrowing speculatively. "I can just see you in your surplice.... Quite handsome." Then, embarrassed, she looked away.

He was gratified and amused by her spontaneous candour, but compelled to point out, "How one looks in a surplice has little to do with how well one performs one's churchly duties."

"Which good understanding on your part makes me all the more convinced that you would have been an excellent vicar!" Miss Clarke shot back. "Still, looking well in your surplice could not have harmed your popularity amongst the petticoat set!"

Julian laughed out loud, then checked himself as Peter stirred restlessly. When Peter resettled himself and was lying still again, Julian said, "Miss Clarke, you are a parcel of diverse delights, one moment delivering me of a sermon and the next moment speaking in cant which would twist your papa's spleen!"

"And you, my Lord Ashton," she said with a wavering smile, "are just as much a bundle of inconsistencies. You claim yourself to be an uncaring man, yet you've shown a plenitude of kindness in the past couple days since I met you. You were gracious to my parents, forgiving and playfully tolerant of my brothers and sister, tenderly watchful and loving of your nephew, kind to your servants and mine, and to the Tuppers, whom you don't even know. And as for Sebastian, what a fortunate cat to have crossed paths with *you!* I daresay few noblemen are kind enough to take a miscreant cat under their protection.''

"I must confess, Miss Clarke, I did it all to impress you," he said teasingly. He did do it for her, he suddenly realized, but not to impress her. Rather she inspired him to do good simply for the pleasure it gave him. Good God, what a frightening thought!

"Please don't begin again with the flummery, my lord," Miss Clarke begged him, grown suddenly very shy and withdrawn. "You promised!"

"I apologize," he said to put her mind at ease. Then, briskly, "Now, who shall take the first watch?"

Lily protested, but Lord Ashton insisted that they take turns through the night in sitting with Peter, or neither of them would be worth a penny for a beggar on the morrow. Lily finally relented, having decided that Lord Ashton was as stubborn as a mule, but of equal conviction that he was entirely in the right.

After bathing Peter's face with a handkerchief soaked in lavender-water and coaxing the twitchy patient to sip a bit of barley broth, Lily lay down on the truckle-bed and tried to sleep. Miraculously, she did, and much longer than she had intended. She awoke to

Peter moaning and Lord Ashton trying to rearrange his nephew's pillow so that the poor, feverish fellow was more comfortable. A hopeless task, it seemed. Peter appeared to be destined for an entire night of half deliriums and unrestful slumber.

Lily rose from the truckle-bed and immediately went to Peter's side. Working together to calm and soothe the agitated patient, Lily and the viscount were finally successful. When Peter's sleeping was relatively peaceful, Lily moved to the washstand and tidied herself in front of the mirror situated atop it. Then, philosophically deciding that her hair was hopeless and the creases in her dress quite permanent, she sat down in the chair next to Peter's bed. Lord Ashton draped a quilt about her shoulders, and she trembled when his hands rested there a little longer than necessary.

"It's rather chilly in here. I'll stoke up the fire," he said.

Peering over her shoulder, Lily looked up at him. "And then you'll lie down?" Lord Ashton's hair was tousled, as if he'd raked a worried hand through it several times. His neckcloth was undone and his jacket had been discarded. In his unbuttoned waistcoat and with his shirtsleeves rolled up to just below his elbows, he looked attractively rumpled. There was a slight shadow of whiskers on his lean jaw. Lily had a strong urge to stroke his face with an open palm and see just how stubbly his chin was.

"No, I can't sleep. I'll keep you company."

"That was not our arrangement!" Lily objected. "We were supposed to spell each other. You'll be exhausted in the morning!"

"In my opinion, there's nothing more exhausting than tossing about on a bed trying to sleep when you know you won't. I should rather sit up all night." Then he moved to the fireplace to poke at the embers and set another log on the grate.

Lily knew there was no point in arguing and, in truth, she hadn't the energy. Besides, if he kept his promise and did not talk fustian, she would be glad of his company. Peter's feverish condition was frightening her a little, and if he thrashed about and tried to get out of bed during the night, Lord Ashton's strength would certainly be useful.

The rest of the night passed quickly. There was really no opportunity for the viscount to talk fustian, since they were both of them very much involved in nursing Peter, who tossed and moaned and struggled intermittently till nearly dawn. Then, as the sun broke over the distant hillside, he seemed to take a turn for the better. He lay completely quiet for the first time since midnight and his upper lip shimmered with perspiration. The fever had broken.

The two of them stood over the bed, utterly exhausted and dishevelled from wrestling the invalid through his deliriums and forcing him to take his medicine. And from worry. Lily turned to look at the viscount and was warmed by the expression of relief and love on his face as he stared at his nephew. When he turned to look at her, a shared happiness permeated the air between them, connecting them like two ends of a rainbow.

"Thank God, he'd going to be all right!" whispered Lord Ashton hoarsely. "I can admit to you now that I've been entertaining the worst fears!"

"As was I," Lily admitted.

"We'll stay at the inn till after noon. There will still be enough daylight to get us home before dinner. I think Peter should not be moved for a few hours. He needs the rest. And so do you! Go to your room and refresh yourself and sleep at least two hours. Peter's out of danger now, so there's no reason for you to stay. Then, when you have recovered a little from this travail, you can sit with Peter while I retire to Pleshy's room, there to be restored to my usual state of order by placing myself in his capable hands! I shudder to think what he'll say when he sees me!"

"If he is as wonderful as Janet says he is, he will understand completely!"

"So that's how the wind blows, eh?" chuckled Lord Ashton. "I hope Janet is right about Pleshy in this instance. Now, do you go to your chamber immediately! The sooner you rest and refresh yourself, the sooner might I. But do not—I hope you understand me on this point, Miss Clarke!—do *not* return to this chamber till at least two hours have transpired. *Do* you understand me?"

"Of course, my lord," she murmured, moving to the door and letting herself out. She snatched another glance at the viscount before she closed the door behind her. He was smiling at her. To her he looked even more attractive in his state of disarray than in his impeccable evening clothes. And the compassionate nature of his exertions during the night, which had made such a charming mess of his person and clothes, was the most attractive aspect of all. *Yes, my lord,* she thought to herself. *I believe I begin to understand you very well!*

IT WAS HALF PAST NOON. The morning had passed in the blink of an eye. Lily had bathed and changed her clothes, and her hair was pulled into a tight knot at the back of her head. She had adjured Janet to dispense with any effort to create a fancy style, but to simply pull all the tresses together into a neat little knot.

Janet had seemed a bit miffed at first, rightly attributing Lily's reluctance for a modish style to the fact that Janet was not as yet adept at dressing hair. But Lily hadn't the patience that morning to allow her to practise. She just desired neatness and plainness in her appearance. She wanted to look sensible, thereby (hopefully) transferring that much-needed custom to her rebellious brain and heart. Lord Ashton had impressed her so much last night, he'd been so wonderful in every way, she knew that it would take very little more to make her heel over ears in love with him. That would not be sensible at all.

Lily stood in the entrance hall of the small inn waiting for Lord Ashton to descend the stairs with

Peter. She had put on her grey coat and bonnet and was pulling on her mittens. She heard the clatter of hooves outside and turned to watch through a small window as the coach that carried Janet, Pleshy and Belle left the courtyard. Lord Ashton had ordered them to go on ahead so as to alert the Ashton household that Peter was soon to arrive.

It was a beautiful, clear day, with no clouds in sight. She imagined that the air was quite cold and crisp and hoped that Peter would not feel the chill too much. He had eaten a reasonably adequate breakfast and sipped some chicken broth for lunch. There was no trace of the fever left. His pulse was slow and steady. He was not very energetic or talkative, but he seemed calm and certainly more rested than the day before.

The black-and-gray berline pulled up in front of the inn, and, at the same moment, Lily heard the stairs creak behind her. She turned and watched as Lord Ashton carried Peter down the stairs, with Sebastian following, well out of the way of his lordship's feet.

Just as on that first stop in Kennington, Lily was deeply moved at the sight of Lord Ashton's gentle handling of his nephew. Not only had he to be careful of Peter's fragile body, but also of the young man's pride. So he was cheerful and nonchalant when he carried Peter, making it seem more of a game between bosom bows than an actual necessity.

Lord Ashton's chin was no longer stubbly. He was shaved and bathed and looked fresh as a nosegay in his brown jacket and pinstriped waistcoat. His hair reflected the golden sunshine that spilled through the sheer drapes at the windows and his aureate eyes— though a trifle weary-looking—returned her scrutiny with an amused twinkle. When she encountered that look, she felt the colour rise in her cheeks.

"Open the door, Miss Clarke, won't you?" he called out cheerfully when he had almost reached the last step.

Lily rushed to do his bidding, chiding herself for not thinking to do it in the first place. But the man had such an effect on her that she was not always thinking as she ought. As they passed through the door, Peter smiled at her. "Good afternoon, Lily. Are you ready to meet my mama?"

"Why, certainly, Peter. Why shouldn't I be?" she returned, exiting through the inn door and dashing ahead of them to open the coach door, then remembering belatedly that they had a groom to do that. So, instead, she stood to the side and watched, fascinated, as Lord Ashton adroitly manoeuvred his own very large frame and Peter's inside. She stepped in behind them and immediately set about the task of tucking Peter's blankets all about him and positioning the hot brick at his feet to maximize its warming benefits. This initial settling in took a few minutes, and the coach had already moved through the small town and was in the countryside by the time Peter was truly comfortable.

"I thought you might be a little anxious about meeting her, you know," Peter said, returning to the subject of Lily's inevitable encounter with his mother. He smiled knowingly.

Lily raised her brows, perfectly understanding him, but choosing not to show it. "I should only be anxious if she found some fault with the way I've cared for you. I hope I have been a good nurse to you, Peter. Your uncle approves of me. Why shouldn't your mama?"

Peter clicked his tongue with exasperation. "Oh, Lily, you know very well I'm not talking about *that!* Of course Mama will think you've done a bang-up job. As to your suitability as a nurse, that goes without saying. But..." He paused and smiled hopefully. "I thought you might be wanting her approval of you in another, er, position."

Lily's eyes met the viscount's for a brief moment. His expression was a mixture of curiosity and concern. Doubtless he was watching with interest to see how she dealt with Peter's persistence in thinking himself in love with her. She turned and fixed her gaze on the dense forest-like scenery outside the window on her side of the coach. They were already several miles from town. Nonchalantly, she said, "I do hope your mama likes me, Peter, but not for any special reason."

Peter made a scoffing noise. "Oh, Lily! Why do you pretend as though you don't understand me? You know how I feel about you—"

Peter's eloquent professions of love were curtailed by the coach stopping very suddenly, in fact more abruptly than when they'd stopped to help the Tuppers. Lily was propelled from her seat, but, thankfully, was caught at the waist by Lord Ashton, who somehow managed to maintain his balance and his seat. Thankfully, Peter had not lost his seat but had merely jerked backward against the carriage squabs. However, Sebastian was not so fortunate. Once again the unsuspecting feline was hurled through the air and onto the floor, leaving in his wake a shower of yellow fur. There he huddled, his tail twitching back and forth as the carriage came to a halt.

"Oh, dear," said Lily, barely able to breathe or speak from the pressure of Lord Ashton's strong arms about her waist. "Is there another carriage off the road?"

But judging by the agitated shouts of Jem, the coachman, and the string of epithets spewed out by Bob, the groom, the reason for their sudden stop was not nearly so commonplace as a broken carriage wheel. Then Lily heard a strange voice bellow, "Stand and deliver!"

CHAPTER NINE

JULIAN QUICKLY RELEASED Miss Clarke and reached inside his greatcoat pocket. The pistol was there, of course, but he just wanted to reassure himself for a moment that they were not completely defenceless. He would not use the weapon unless it were absolutely necessary. Facing off against several men with short-barreled but deadly blunderbusses with a small pistol as his only weapon of defence would not be at all prudent. But if one of them so much as looked cross-eyed at Miss Clarke, he'd put the fellow to bed with a shovel without the slightest twinge of conscience, whatever might the consequences be! On the other hand, possibly there was only one thief on the road today. So far, he could detect the sound of only a single set of hooves on the frost-hardened ground.

"Highwaymen!" Peter said excitedly.

"Or highway*man,*" Julian suggested.

"But if there is only one of them, how did he manage to stop the carriage without your man firing any shots?" asked Lily. "It's broad daylight outside, too! He must be quite desperate to attack a guarded coach without cover of darkness!" While Miss Clarke's forehead was faintly creased in a concerned expression, she was maintaining her composure with amazing sang-froid.

"Hush! Our questions will soon be answered," whispered Julian, straining to hear what was going on outside. The carriage rocked gently to and fro. "Jem and Bob have been ordered off the box. I'm sure he's already taken their shotguns away from them."

Now a gruff voice was heard to say, "Over there by the tree, and nothin' 'avey-cavey or I'll use these 'ere poppers, make no doubt!"

"Why don't we storm 'em?" Peter proposed enthusiastically. Then, as if he'd suddenly remembered that he had barely the strength to walk, much less to storm somebody, he looked chagrined and said mournfully, "Stupid idea! Forgot I was such a weakling!"

"It wouldn't serve, anyway," said Julian consideringly. "Though it irks me to let the fellow get away with this robbery, it will be better to cooperate with him than to endanger Miss Clarke. If he offers no violence, neither shall we. Now he'll order us to vacate the carriage."

True to Julian's predictions, presently the voice was directed towards them. "You swells in th' carriage, one at a time, out you go! And if'n you've got a popper on your person, throw it through the window now, 'cause if'n I sees so much as a glimpse o' somethin' what even looks like a shooter, I'll put an 'ole in your 'eart."

Miss Clarke turned to Julian, for the first time seeming rather agitated. "You had better give him the pistol! Surely he'll make you empty your pockets, and when he sees the weapon, he'll shoot you!"

Julian shook his head. "No. Then we'd be completely defenceless. I won't relinquish it."

"Out, I say!" bellowed the highwayman, obviously growing impatient.

Turning to Miss Clarke, Julian whispered, "Stay inside the carriage unless I tell you otherwise," then he opened the carriage door and stepped out.

Julian's first view of the robber was rather daunting. Now he understood how the man had single-handedly stopped the carriage. First of all, he must have caught Bob and Jem unawares, then stunned them with his immense size and aimed a shotgun at them before they'd retrieved their wits. The man was built like a mountain! Julian pitied the poor horse required to sit this huge fellow's considerable weight, especially when he observed that the horse appeared underfed.

By Julian's estimation, the man was at least six feet five inches tall and weighed over seventeen stone, most of which was sheer brute muscle. His dark hair and smooth face framed with a beard suggested his age to be no more than Julian's. He had a scarf tied round his head and over his eyes, with two slits to see through. His buckskin breeches and coat were worn and dirty. He had not the dapper appearance of some seasoned thieves, nor had he the confident air. Julian's eyes narrowed. Perhaps the man's bravery in waylaying the carriage by himself could be better described as foolhardiness. Perhaps this highwayman was still inexperienced. This knowledge gave them a bit of an edge.

Julian stepped forward and lifted his hands, saying calmly, "Well, here I am! Now what?" Out of the corner of his eye, he could see Jem and Bob roped to a nearby tree, both of them looking cross as crabs. He tried to ignore his own rising indignation and affixed his gaze unswervingly on the eyes behind the thief's scarf.

The highwayman's own gaze shifted uneasily, as if he were disconcerted by Julian's steady scrutiny. "They's other coves in th' carriage. I don't want no rigs ner flashy 'eroics, you 'ere?" He raised his blunderbuss menacingly, but Julian noticed that his hand shook. The highwayman had Jem's shotgun in his other hand, and Bob's was tucked inside a sort of saddle-bag.

Julian gestured towards the carriage. "There's no one in there besides a young lady and my nephew, who is too ill to move. Let them stay where they are and I'll fetch their valuables for you," he offered with dry cordiality. "Though how you can be such a scoundrel as to crib the ready from a defenceless woman and the man she's nursing because of a wound he suffered at Waterloo, I cannot conceive!"

Through the slightly opened carriage window, Julian heard Miss Clarke's sharp intake of breath. No doubt she thought he'd gone completely noddy, baiting the fellow so.

"Times is 'ard fer everybody," growled the dick turpin. "'Specially for th' poor fellows what fought in th' war!"

Suddenly Julian noticed the man's boots. They were military issue. This highwayman had fought for King and Country as well. Was he, like so many of the returning enlisted men, unable to feed himself and his family with honest, paying employment?

"Yes, times are hard," Julian agreed. "As I said, my nephew, Peter, here, was wounded at Waterloo. But do you know why he's so ill now?"

The highwayman gave a frustrated grunt and scanned the area for intruders with a sharp swivel of his head. "I'm sorry for yer nephew, but I can't stand about 'ere all day listenin' t'you pitchin' me gammon! How should I know what you're tellin' me is the truth? And it don't make no difference, anyhow!"

"Doesn't it?" Julian challenged. "After Peter recovered enough to cross the channel to Dover, as he awaited transportation home he was set upon by a footpad, hit over the head and relieved of all his blunt and all his clothing, as well. He was left to freeze and die by the roadside. Quite a hero's welcome, wasn't it?"

The man's sneer wavered. He looked nonplussed momentarily, then rallied his defences, saying, "I ain't the villain what made your nephew nearly slip 'is wind! I don't want to 'urt no one. I jest want your valuables and with no more gabble-grindin'!'' During this speech, the highwayman had become increasingly perturbed, jerking his shooters about like an escapee from Bedlam. His skinny horse whinnied and tossed its head restlessly.

Julian had tried to reason with the man, but to no avail. He was resigned to losing his money and his watchfob, but was seriously displeased with the notion of giving up his signet ring. He thought of the pistol in his pocket and briefly considered retrieving it, but the idea of risking Miss Clarke's or Peter's life over the loss of a paltry piece of jewelry, despite its sentimental significance, was unthinkable.

Julian began to pull off his ring. Might as well do the most painful thing first. . . .

"Oh, for heaven's sake, what a to-do!"

Julian jerked round and discovered Miss Clarke stepping out of the carriage, with Peter trying to grasp her arm as he exclaimed incoherent words of protest and frustration. "Do quit grabbing, Peter, for you won't stop me!" she advised him at last, gently twisting her wrist out of his weak grip, then firmly closing the door behind her. Peter pressed his nose against the window glass, staring out with an agonized and apologetic expression. Lily paid him no heed, straightened up, tucked a stray wisp of hair under her plain poke bonnet, and placed her fists on her hips.

"Miss Clarke," Julian began ominously, his insides twisting with trepidation for the danger the foolish girl was exposing herself to unnecessarily. "I told you to stay in the carriage!"

"Well, I don't have to do everything you tell me, do I?" she countered irascibly. "I'm not your wife or your sister, or anything of the sort! I'm an unmarried woman with a mind of my own! And when I perceived that you'd given up on this fellow, I found I could not sit still another moment! Why, you had almost convinced him!"

"Lily!" Julian ground out. "Go back to the carriage before I—"

Miss Clarke raised her chin haughtily. "Who gave you permission to use my Christian name, Lord Ashton? And why do you suppose I should do as *you* tell me and scamper back into the carriage, when *this* gentleman—the one holding a weapon, I might add— has asked that I step outside? I'm only doing what I deem as most prudent!"

"She's a right one, my lord," said the highwayman approvingly, staring at Miss Clarke with a rather bemused expression. "She knows it ain't polite-like t'jaw away the whole mornin' and waste a fella's time. Now, girly, take his lordship's valuables and bring 'em here!"

Once again the delicate chin lifted haughtily. "I will *not!*"

"Miss Clarke!" Julian lamented, kneading his forehead with agitated fingers. "You're not dealing with an innkeep who likes to abuse cats here! The man has a shotgun, for the love of heaven!"

"And I'm not afeared t'use it!" warned the bounder with hopeful bravado, as if he felt he was losing control of the situation—which, indeed, he was.

"I don't believe you for a minute," Miss Clarke informed him with flashing eyes. "You're not the sort of man to shoot a defenceless person. You said just a moment ago that you didn't want to hurt anyone! You were a soldier, weren't you, sir?"

"So what if I was?" he said bitterly. "What good did it do me?"

"It taught you how very precious life is, didn't it? After dodging bullets yourself and seeing your compatriots die, you must realize how very important it is to preserve life, not take it senselessly!"

"What's senseless is me wife and four chil'ren goin' without the necessaries, when I've the back and the will t'work 'ard!"

"If that's the case, why haven't you found employment?" Lord Ashton enquired, unobtrusively placing himself between the man's line of fire and Miss Clarke.

"You wouldn't understand, your lordship," sneered the highwayman. "You've never 'ad to worry a day in your pretty life, I'll wager. For your 'igh-and-mighty's information, they's no work to be 'ad 'ereabouts. Now shut yer trap, and 'and over the ready!"

"Oh, dear," murmured Miss Clarke, "you *are* being mulish! And impolite, too! Do you find this sort of work rewarding, Mr.... What did you say your name was?"

The highwayman wheezed with laughter, his huge chest heaving beneath his tattered coat. "What do you take me for, miss, a Johnny-raw? I ain't goin' t'tell you my name!"

"Then tell me your story! I assure you, sir, I'm most interested and deeply stirred by your plight. You haven't been doing this sort of thing very long, have you?"

"Don't insult him, my dear," advised Julian, as he noticed the highwayman stiffen. This whole incident was fast taking on the unreal qualities of a dream. Who ever imagined that the fellow would have been deterred this long from his evil-doing by a slip of a chit's well-intended moralizing? But deter him she had, and perhaps he wasn't even offended by her intimation that he was a novice at dodgey activities.

"This is the first time I've held up a coach," confessed the highwayman at last, after a reflective pause of several moments.

"I thought as much," said Miss Clarke with satisfaction. "Now *do,* if you please, put down your shotguns! I dislike looking into those black barrels worse than anything!"

The highwayman sat up straighter, and lifted and aimed one of the guns—straight at Julian's heart. "I ain't no fool! I ain't goin' to give m'self up to the 'ands of the law and find m'self strung up at t'gallows!"

Miss Clarke released an exasperated breath. "No one's going to turn you over to the constable, my good man! You haven't stolen anything, have you? Put down your guns and go your way, and promise me that you won't do such a stupid thing again!" she admonished like a lecturing nanny.

"What about *'im?*" said the highwayman, gesturing towards Julian. "'ow do I know *'e* won't set the law after me at the next village? I don't exactly disappear in a crowd. They'd snabble me and I wouldn't have nothin' t'show for it, neither!"

"I have no intention of sending the law after you," Julian assured him in a beleaguered voice. "I've much better things to do today, like getting my nephew home to his mother! Christmas draws nigh and I have an aversion to being skinned alive. If you're going to rob us, do it swiftly! Or if you're going to give up your life of crime, please do that in a similarly expeditious manner, if you please!"

"My lord," said Miss Clarke, turning to Julian with a remonstrative air, "you must see that the fellow feels himself at daggers drawn! He obviously doesn't want to rob us, but the alternative is not very attractive, either! How will he feed his family?"

Julian watched while Miss Clarke pondered deeply. He felt like a man awaiting his sentencing from the magistrate. But he knew what his fate would be, even before her eyes lit up and she turned to him with an eager expression, saying, "I have a capital idea, my lord! Your estate is a large establishment, requiring many hands to keep it running smoothly, I daresay. Do you suppose...?"

"First you foist upon me a miscreant cat who is quite worthless—"

"Never say so!" interrupted Miss Clarke indignantly. "Sebastian has been a comfort to Peter!"

"Then you thrust me headlong into the middle of a family argument and saddle me with another servant, who, for all I know, may or may not be the least bit deedy about the house—"

"That was your idea entirely!" Miss Clarke reminded him.

"And now you are hinting that I had ought to interest myself in the plight of this ruffian, who, at this very moment, has a gun aimed at my chest! Do you want me to hire him for the stables, Miss Clarke, or the farm? Or maybe he could replace Mr. Beedle as majordomo of Ashton House? Come along, Miss Clarke, out with it! Why don't you tell me *exactly* what you want and quit beating about the bush!"

"Goodness, we're in a bit of a twitch, aren't we, my lord?" she said loftily. "But if you must know what I was thinking particularly, it is this. I had thought you might make the highwayman—" She turned to the astounded but deeply interested would-be criminal and demanded, "You *must* tell me your name! I can't continue to speak of you as 'the highwayman!' It's so awkward."

"My name's Bickford, miss. Norton Bickford," he said automatically, his guns forgotten and drooping in his hands, the muzzles pointed to the ground.

Miss Clarke smiled approvingly. "Thank you, Mr. Bickford. As I was saying," she continued, turning back to Julian with an officious air, "you could make Mr. Bickford one of your tenants, allowing him to put off paying his rent till he's made a profit, or possibly set him to work at odd jobs about the estate to earn the needful. It would be a lot of hard work at first, Mr. Bickford, but you appear very hearty. I'm sure you could do it!"

Now Mr. Bickford's arms fell to his sides. Clearly he was shocked and disbelieving, but the hint of hope aborning in his barrel-like chest was evident in his softened expression. "What say you to such an addle-pated idea, my lord?" he asked.

Julian sighed deeply and his mouth twisted into a rather lopsided grin. "I won't even consider such a proposition—"

Mr. Bickford's face crumpled.

Julian extended his open palm. "Until you hand over those pistols, all three of them, if you please! Staring down the muzzle of a gun is likely to put anybody in a 'twitch' you know!"

Mr. Bickford frowned at Julian, then stared at his weapons consideringly. Then he turned back to Julian, a glimmer of fear in his black eyes. "Can I trust you, I wonder?"

"Certainly not," Julian informed him briskly. He hooked a thumb at Miss Clarke. "But you can trust *her*, and it appears she has the stronger will between us. All shall be done just as Miss Clarke suggested. It just so happens that I've a small property which needs a tenant, and I don't mind waiting for the rent for a little while.''

Mr. Bickford shook his head dolefully as he sent his horse mincing forward and bent down to hand the guns, stock first, to Julian. ''I've gone daft, I expect,'' he muttered faintly. ''Or else I've met my guardian angel!''

Julian took the guns and said airily, ''If Miss Clarke's your guardian angel, you must be prepared to share her! It seems she has a prodigious quantity of human beings to watch over. Now, how shall we go about this thing we've undertook? Mr. Bickford, do you live nearby?''

''Aye, my lord,'' Mr. Bickford replied, gesturing in a westward direction. '''Cross the river in Churt.''

''Did your wife know how you meant to employ yourself today, Mr. Bickford?''

Mr. Bickford looked shamefaced. ''No. And it would kill 'er if she'd knowed about it. You won't tell 'er, will you, my lord?''

''No, of course not!'' Julian scoffed, thoughtfully rubbing his chin. ''I won't be able to make your wife's acquaintance this day, for I'd not get Peter home in time for dinner with his mother if we went so far out of the way. I'm just wondering how you'll explain meeting me and suddenly becoming my tenant. Hmm. This will require some subtlety. Climb off your horse, Mr. Bickford, and allow me time to think.''

Julian caught Miss Clarke looking at him and said, "Don't tell me not to concoct a lie, because I have no choice in this instance! We'll stick as close to the truth as we can, but eliminate certain facts which might distress Mrs. Bickford." He turned back to Mr. Bickford. "Then, once we've agreed on a story to suit, I'll give you the direction to Ashton House. To set your mind at ease that my intentions are honourable and not likely to be forgotten as soon as you ride out of sight, I will also supply you with a written note of agreement to be brought with you to my estate within the week. Or can your family pack up and come sooner, do you think?"

Mr. Bickford assured Julian that the sooner they left the God-forsaken village of Churt, the happier he'd be.

Then, bethinking himself of other possible contingencies, Julian pulled Mr. Bickford out of earshot of the others and asked, "Have you food and such to sustain you till your move? Do you need a wagon to convey your belongings?"

No, he said to the first, yes to the second. Julian gave him some money, which Mr. Bickford nearly wept over, and then left the man to compose himself while he fetched pen and paper from a small leather portmanteau inside the carriage and scribbled directions and promises in an elegant hand. Miss Clarke was uncharacteristically unobtrusive during these proceedings, seemingly satisfied to merely watch. She had such an odd little expression on her face, too, one that Julian could not fathom at all.

Mr. Bickford blinked over the paper, admitting that he could not read a word of it, but was inclined to believe that Julian had written just what he'd said he would. A hard, more cunning part of his mind told him the whole thing was a hum, or a dream, and mayhap a constable would somehow have been alerted and would be waiting to shackle him at the door of his humble cottage. But, as he said, just on the chance that Miss Clarke *was* his guardian angel, and because he *did* have a constitutional dislike of robbing people at gunpoint, he decided to take Julian at his word. My Lord Ashton was a gentleman, after all, and if one could not believe the word of an English gentleman, then the world had indeed gone all to pieces, he concluded eloquently.

After further confidential conversation between them, concocting a story to suit, Mr. Bickford obligingly untied Julian's henchmen, who, though they had seen and heard the whole incident, still harboured some resentment and mistrust towards the beefy highwayman. Julian watched his latest charitable undertaking lumber about, the fellow looking as meek as a lamb. He did not yet trust the highwayman, either, and he only hoped that Mr. Bickford would not take a sudden turn for the worse and decide to slit their throats.

By now Julian was thoroughly convinced that he'd gone mad to so personally involve himself in the man's life. What had got into him to have become so philanthropic of a sudden?

But he knew. He knew that Miss Clarke—Lily, as he should rather choose to call her—had exerted her influence over him to such a degree that the icy fortress of indifference he'd built up as a protection over the years was fast melting. The heating source had originated somewhere in the region of his heart and, like a deadly virus, had run rampant through his bloodstream till he was quite overcome with the fever of humanitarianism.

He now realized that the condition had been creeping up on him for the past three days, perhaps since the moment he'd set foot inside that beatific bedlam, the Whitfield Vicarage. It had been a positive shock to his system to encounter such enthusiasm in Lily and such genuine goodwill in her and all her family. Immersed as he'd been in the shallow pursuits of Town life, he'd been comfortably insulated from the difficulties and pathos of the common man, and the challenges they faced, especially after the war.

Developing an awareness and a sense of responsibility for the lives of others less fortunate than himself foretold a certain amount of trouble and pain for Julian's future. But wasn't it better to feel pain than nothing at all? And, along with the pain, he knew he'd feel a measure of satisfaction for helping out where he was able. And he'd experience other emotions more keenly, as well. Emotions like love, for instance.

They resumed their journey, with Mr. Bickford riding his horse alongside the carriage till he was required to cross the river to Churt. At Julian's request, Nort, as he urged them to call him, removed the scarf that had covered his head and eyes, revealing a mass of black, curly hair, and tufted eyebrows that crawled across his forehead like woolly caterpillars to kiss at a point just above the bridge of his generously sized nose.

Julian gave Nort's gun into the keeping of Bob, explaining that the weapon would be returned when Nort arrived at Ashton House with his family. Nort submitted to this plan without argument. Julian's own pistol was kept right where it had always been—in his pocket. For while they had talked Nort out of his intention to rob them, Julian was aware that most highwaymen were ruthless outlaws capable of much worse than merely robbing them. Unlike his brother Richard, Julian was a practical man, awake to the realities of life and determined that if his fate *was* to be a philanthropist, he would still make certain that he used his head to as much purpose as he used his heart.

His heart. He slid a covert glance at Lily. Since Nort's addition to their travelling circus, Lily had been as still as a mouse. An ironic comparison, perhaps, since she disdained rodents so very much. But, suffice it to say, she'd been completely silent, and much of the time stared out of the window at the crystalline beauty of an English winter idyll. But she did not appear to be appreciating the beauty before her; rather she was deep in sober reflection.

Back to his heart. It ached a little now, watching her, wondering what complexities of philanthropy weighed heavily in her thoughts. Was she thinking about Nort's family, fretting over the idea of four children gone so long without enough milk to help them grow tall and strong?

He wanted to soothe away that tiny crease of worry between her brows. He wanted to take her in his arms and comfort her. . . .

Julian moved restlessly, finally looking out his own window and probably seeing as little of the view as did Lily. He examined his heart with the thoroughness of a nit-picking monkey from the London Menagerie, and realized he wanted to do much more than comfort Lily. He wanted to crush the little baggage to his chest and cover her face with kisses. He wanted to protect her and extricate her from all the scrapes she'd doubtless fling herself into with regularity throughout her life.

Then, once she had done her daily good deed, he wanted to drag her home at night to his own bed, therein to redirect all that goodwill and enthusiasm into the very satisfying activity called lovemaking. For he loved her.

He did not consider their difference in fortunes. He had enough money to secure much more than the necessities of life. And while Lily did not move in the same tonnish circles as did Julian, he realized how unnecessary those people were to his happiness. Fundamentally, Julian felt a much stronger kinship with this little vicar's daughter than to any of his London cronies and flirts. But, reflecting on his upbringing, destined as he had been for the clergy, he realized falling in love with Lily was probably the most natural thing he could have done.

Now came the rub. Peter loved her, too, or at least thought he did. Worse than that, Julian knew, was the fact that Lily had a very poor opinion of *him*, and probably hadn't the slightest inclination to fall in love with such a good-for-nothing fellow! However, he wasn't going to let that stop him! Besides, there were times when he thought she might not exactly hold him in complete aversion.... For example, when he'd almost kissed her....

Lily had said she would stay at Ashton House for a day or two if necessary to get Peter settled in. Julian determined that in that short amount of time he would try to make a little indentation on her heart and somehow prove to her that though he was a sinner and a cynic, he wasn't *all* bad!

CHAPTER TEN

LILY THOUGHT HER HEART would explode. She had never felt so full of diverse feelings, and all of them bumping about inside of her, demanding to be understood and somehow acted upon. But Lily hadn't the slightest idea how to act upon feelings she'd never experienced before in her lifetime. For they all had to do with Julian, Lord Ashton, Lion of the ton, self-described sinner and cynic. In Lily's eyes, he was a man whose character was a delightful mixture of droll humour, practicality and an innate, empathetic love for and tolerance of the common man—and all this despite the tragedies he'd had to endure! But he saw himself quite differently.

Lily almost wished she shared the deprecating view he had of himself. Perhaps then she wouldn't see him as the perfect man. She was quite sure that in his eyes *she* was a perfect nuisance! If they were to marry— quite an absurd, wishful thought, of course!—she would be forever putting him in situations where he would be compelled to use that wonderful ability he possessed of mixing compassion with good sense to come up with a minor miracle. As in the case of Nort.

But, at this point in his life, perhaps Lord Ashton had rather not be expected to create miracles on a daily basis. It would be too fatiguing.

Lily sighed and reached across the carriage to pet Sebastian, curled up at Peter's feet. The feline opened his slumberous eyes to narrow crescents and peered at her for a moment, then closed them again. Peter did not stir at all; he'd been asleep for the past hour. With dusk fast approaching, they were within easy distance of Ashton House.

As she leaned forward, she heard Lord Ashton shift a little in his seat. She could feel his eyes upon her like burning coals, but she dared not return his look for fear of exposing her yearning to be held in his arms and to have his lips pressed to hers. Oh, dear, *what* would Papa say of such intemperate thoughts? But a part of her knew that her mother had probably felt— and still felt—those identical yearnings for her father. It was a natural consequence of falling in love. There, she'd admitted it. She was in love.

"We have arrived."

Lily started and turned towards Lord Ashton, thankful of the gathering shadows which must be obscuring her face just as effectively as they obscured the viscount's. He was a grey blur in a dark high-crowned beaver, his striking features indistinct, but he still exuded a vital presence. "We have?" was her intelligent reply.

"Yes, in about two minutes we'll turn in at the lodge gates. I wish it were lighter outside so that you could see better. The countryside round and about Ashton House is beautiful.''

"I'm sure it is," Lily murmured. She turned again to look out her window and saw inky outlines of tree branches against a pinkish-grey sky. Then, on the right side of the road, a tall lodge tower emerged from the twilight gloom. The gate was open and they turned neatly in, but the sway of the carriage awakened Peter.

As if he knew exactly where they were, Peter quickly became alert and sat up, nudging Sebastian gently out of the way as he swung his legs to the floor. "We're here!" he stated in a voice vibrating with suppressed excitement. "I think I can smell the Christmas punch already!"

Lord Ashton laughed. "Then you're still asleep, Peter! We've only just turned in at the gates and are going down the avenue. Look!"

Peter needed no further encouragement. He pushed his face as close as possible to the carriage window glass and stared out. "Dear, dear, Ashton House!" he said fondly. "How good it is to see your lawns and gardens again, even though it is nearly dark outside and the middle of winter! During the war, I dreamed of Ashton House as much as I did my own estate in Derbyshire, Lily," Peter told her, turning with a boyish, confiding smile she could just barely see in the dim light from the window. "I spent many happy summers here mucking about the grounds and playing shuttlecock and battledore with the Cavendish twins, Lucinda and Lizzy. Are they still about, Julian?''

"Still about and still unmarried," Lord Ashton replied drily. "Most probably nursing their tendres for you, Peter." Lord Ashton spoke into the darkness in the general direction of Lily. "They were both of them in love with him, you see."

"Were they indeed?" Lily said, interested and happy to have something to talk about that would divert her from her own painful musings. "Are they nice girls, Peter?"

"Better than 'nice!' They're *jolly* girls, and pretty, too!" Peter answered emphatically. "Almost as good as a regular chum, since they're not averse to a little horseplay!"

"His mama and I expected him to hang up the ladle with one of them, but it seemed he could never make up his mind between the two," Julian further explained.

"It wasn't at all a *settled* thing, you know," Peter defended himself. "And now they are going on to three-and-twenty. Positively on the shelf! I hope I may not have been the reason for *that!* Either of them would have made a fine wife, but I wasn't ready to marry then. However, now that the war's over and I've seen a bit of the world, the idea of settling down to one woman suits me just fine! Only, I don't think either Lizzie or Lucinda is the lady for me!" Even though she couldn't see it, Lily could feel Peter's meaningful look directed towards her.

Neither Lily nor Lord Ashton made a reply to Peter's admission. His infatuation with her troubled Lily all the more now that they were ending their journey, because he would probably do something idiotish like declare himself. She wished there was some way to discourage him without hurting him. But then she did not flatter herself to think the hurt would be of long duration, because she knew his affection for her was only a result of their necessary closeness over the past weeks and his gratitude to her for nursing him.

At that moment, Lily decided that for Peter's sake and for hers, she would leave Ashton House the very next morning. The longer she was in his company, the longer he would perhaps delude himself into thinking that they were destined to be together. And the longer she stayed near Lord Ashton, especially in the interesting and personal surroundings of his own home, the more she would become besotted with him.

She could discuss Peter's health with his mother; and certainly Mrs. Wendover, and the many servants at her disposal, could give Peter all the attention he required.

The avenue curved in front of the house, and Lily looked up at a massive stone building with steep gables and tall windows, all of which seemed to be aglow with welcoming candlelight. The snow had pretty much melted, or perhaps Hampshire had not been as inundated by the wet, white precipitation as had the more easterly counties. Their arrival was anticipated, for as soon as they came to a full stop in front of the entrance, they could see that the main door was open wide and several people were staring out. Then one small female figure detached itself from the crowd and ran down the steps. It had to be Peter's mother.

Peter was trembling with expectation by now and he tried to stand up and exit the carriage on his own. Lord Ashton quickly caught him at the elbow and helped him descend the carriage steps, there to be clasped about the waist and squeezed with as much might as Mrs. Wendover could muster.

"Peter! Oh, Peter! I've missed you so!" she exclaimed tearily, pressing her face into the crumpled folds of his neckcloth.

Peter laughed softly and gazed down fondly at his mother's charmingly capped head, patting that confection of lace and muslin with a tender hand. "No more than I've missed you, Mama!"

"Come, Winny, let's get Peter inside and settled on a sofa by the fire," Lord Ashton interjected, probably concerned that he might collapse on the flagstones and mortify himself. "Then you may fuss over him as much as you like!"

Recalled at once to her motherly duties, Winny wiped her eyes and released her loving stranglehold of Peter, laughing self-consciously. "Oh, dear, yes! Come inside at once!"

So far on their trip, Peter had only walked twice unassisted into the inns they'd stopped at for rest and refreshment, allowing himself to be carried all the other times. But Lily knew—and so, apparently, did

Lord Ashton—that Peter would not allow himself to be carried into this particular establishment for all the King's jewels. He undoubtedly wished to show his mama, and all the servants who had gathered in the main hall to welcome him, that he was in fine fettle.

Lily stationed herself to one side of Peter and Julian on the other, lending an arm unobtrusively, allowing Peter to lean on them as he had the need. They walked up the steps and into the hall in this manner, Peter sometimes weaving a bit, other times leaning heavily, once in a while managing a strutting step or two quite without assistance. Lily was proud of his courage and determination. She had no doubt that Peter would recover completely.

The servants smiled and bade Peter respectful "How do you dos," but Lily could see the affection brimming in their eyes, especially from the older servants who must have watched Peter playing battledore and shuttlecock on the front lawn with the Cavendish twins. Peter greeted them by name and grinned as he slowly made his way to the drawing-room. Mrs. Wendover fluttered about like a protective mother hen, her smile sometimes faltering as she observed her son's weakness and his emaciated body. But she remained obstinately cheerful and seemed determined to show Peter nothing but the most optimistic face.

Pleshy and Janet were amongst the crowd of happy servants congregated in the entrance hall, standing close together and beaming. Lily thought it telling that they still seemed a "pair," even with so many other people around. Apparently what had started as a forced togetherness was being continued by them on a perfectly willing basis. Lily dreaded the expedient of having to wrench Janet away from her beloved Pleshy to return to Whitfield on the morrow.

Belle, in a fresh round gown, spanking-clean apron and fetching mob-cap, already blended in quite well with the Ashton servants and appeared to have been readily accepted by them.

At last Peter was on the sofa with a coverlet and a pillow, and with Sebastian, the living hot brick, cuddled against his feet. Peter's face shimmered with perspiration from his efforts and he looked very pale. But the warm, cheerfully bedecked room seemed to help him recover quickly, and after a drink of watered wine and a pastry of mincemeat, he looked much refreshed.

Finally Peter's mother could relax, and she turned to Lily with a smile and extended her hand, saying warmly, "Well, now that we're settled in a little, we can be properly introduced, Miss Clarke! I hope you do not mind my rudeness in quite ignoring you till now, but I was sure you'd agree with me that we must attend to Peter first."

"Indeed, I agree with you completely, Mrs. Wendover," Lily replied graciously.

"You must call me Winny," said Mrs. Wendover, gesturing for Lily to sit down in a comfortable-looking wing chair by the sofa. The furniture was arranged in a cosy circle about the fireplace. "All my friends call me Winny, and you, Miss Clarke, must allow me to count you as a friend. I can never, ever thank you sufficiently for taking such excellent care of my son!"

"Then you must call me Lily," she returned, sitting down. Her coat and bonnet had been taken from her by a servant in the hall as she'd entered, and she felt as though she must look a sight with her wrinkled blue kerseymere dress and flyaway hair. But "Winny's" warm smile and friendly manner made her forget her state of disarray—almost. Considering the long day they'd had, Lord Ashton still looked posy-fresh, and she was sure *she* looked a fright by comparison. He stood behind Winny's chair, which was opposite Lily's, leaning on the back in a brotherly fashion.

Lord Ashton looked very much at home in the elegant, but inviting drawing-room. Most of the furnishings were made of warm cherrywood, the wall tapestries were rich but not ostentatious, and pictures of pleasant country landscapes hung here and there. Lily liked the room very much and admired the good taste of its owner. She sighed and wished he weren't so very wonderful in every respect.

"You are tired, Miss Clarke?" Julian suggested, his keen eyes affixed to Lily. He had observed her every look and mannerism since she'd entered his house. He had caught her little sigh. She displayed a kind of quiet meekness which seemed out of character for her. He hoped she was not intimidated by Ashton House. Certainly Winny couldn't have made her feel shy, for his sister was all amiability and friendliness. Perhaps she *was* just fatigued.

Lily lifted her eyes to his and a shock of awareness trembled in the air between them. She quickly looked down, saying, "I suppose I *am* a little tired."

"Then you must by all means go to bed directly after dinner," admonished Winny, standing up abruptly. "Of course you will wish to freshen up before we dine. I'll have Beedle fetch Julian's capable housekeeper, Mrs. Strand. She'll show you to your bedchamber. I'm sure by now your abigail—Janet, is it?—will have pressed and laid out a change of clothes for you. She's a delightful young woman and has made quite an impression on the other servants already, so Beedle tells me!"

"That Janet rubs along well with the other servants I readily believe," Lily said, chuckling. "But if she has already pressed and laid out my clothes, I shall be more than a little amazed!"

"Oh, you do say?" said Winny with a surprised shake of her head. "But I expect you know her best. And as for the other girl, Belle, I find the story Pleshy has told us about *her* vastly interesting!" She turned to Julian and arched a brow. "It is especially interesting in the way it concerns you, Julian!"

"Tonight I refuse to answer any questions about the past three days," Julian firmly informed his sister, lifting his hands in a dissuasive gesture.

"Uncle Julian has been acting very odd, Mama," Peter offered, yawning behind his hand. "He not only took in Sebastian and Belle, but there's a highway-man named Nort coming to be one of Julian's ten-ants!''

"What?" cried Winny with a start and a nervous laugh. "A highwayman? Julian, what can have come over you?" She looked at her brother as if he'd lost his wits.

"Lily came over him," said Peter with a sleepy smile. "Comes over everyone.... Sweet girl, Lily. An angel..."

Winny looked back and forth between Lily, who had bowed her head modestly, and Julian. Her eyes held a speculative glint. To forestall his sister's obvious awakening of suspicion concerning the state of his heart (Winny apparently understood him better than he thought), Julian nodded his head in Peter's direction, saying, "Gone to sleep. I daresay he'd not be up to sitting at table yet, anyway, Winny—especially tonight."

As Julian had intended, Winny was distracted. She bent a tender, concerned gaze upon her slumbering son and said, "He's so thin! Does he always fall asleep so quickly and in the middle of a conversation?"

Lily stood up and moved to place a comforting hand on Winny's shoulder. "He is worn out by the journey, and yesterday he had a fever. Don't worry! He's better now, but tonight I must tell you everything about his illness and give you the directions and medicine given me by Dr. Payne."

"You can do all that tomorrow, after you've had a decent night's sleep, Lily, er, Miss Clarke," Julian said. "There's no hurry, is there?"

"Well, actually, there is," said Lily, averting her eyes, as a most becoming shade of pink bloomed on her cheeks. She didn't upbraid him for using her Christian name, and he thought the blush she was wearing lovely. "You see, though I know I offered to stay a few days after our arrival, I begin to think it would be better if I left as soon as possible." Lily glanced up briefly, then quickly returned her gaze to some figuring on the carpet she apparently found fascinating.

Julian felt his heart sink. She was leaving! "Miss Clarke, I don't understand—"

Again she looked up, a slight smile trembling on her lips and unmistakable meaning shining in her eyes. "Now that Peter has his mother to take care of him, he doesn't need *me,* my lord!"

"Oh dear, from what I was able to glean from Peter's letter, he'd much rather you stayed, my dear," Mrs. Wendover fretted.

"Precisely, Winny," Julian murmured. Lily was leaving so as not to encourage Peter, or at least that was what she implied. Did he dare to hope that there was another reason for her flustered look and the way she kept wringing her small hands in front of her? Was he a conceited popinjay to believe that she wasn't entirely indifferent to him? He must know!

"Miss Clarke, though you're probably eager to retire to your chamber, do you think I might have a, er, private word with you?"

Lily looked up quickly, an enquiring, puzzled look in her beautiful brown eyes. "A—a *private* word, my lord?"

"Yes, Miss Clarke, if you don't mind," he said kindly, stepping close and cupping her elbow with his hand to lead her from the room. "You will be quite safe, you know, because I intend to take you only so far as the library, two doors down the hall. Winny will stand guard outside if you like, or she may stay in here with Peter, but either way, I think your papa would consider you sufficiently chaperoned."

Winny had been watching and listening with a delighted interest, her suspicions having been confirmed. "I think you will be quite safe, Lily," she said, smiling warmly as Julian led the young lady, unresisting, out of the room.

Julian looked down at Lily and thought she rather had the look of a Christian about to be fed to the lions. He would find the comparison amusing if he weren't so nervous himself about the outcome of their little interview. He had never imagined that a week ago he'd be hanging all his hopes of happiness on this travel-worn little vicar's daughter with wide brown eyes and untidy hair, but she was exactly what he wanted.

It was almost as though he had been looking at the world through a dirty glass, and Lily had come along with all her industrious goodwill and wiped the glass till it was crystal clear. Of course, he still saw the injustices, the poverty, the evil, but on the other hand, he saw the kindness, the hope, and the miracles that were there, too. Most of all, he wanted to be part of that eternal tug of war between good and bad, pulling hard on the side of goodness. In conclusion, just through their short, intense association, Lily had given back to Julian a purpose to his life.

Lily walked the hall in a sort of dream state, for surely she was asleep and dreaming. Why would Lord Ashton... why would *Julian* want to speak to her privately? There had been only one other person in the room to hear whatever he had to say, and that had been his sister, whom he probably felt more comfortable with than anyone else in the world. What did he wish to keep private from *her?* And if the conversation was to be about Peter, certainly his mother ought to be included. But Winny did not appear affronted by their departure; in fact she'd been smiling when they left the room.

Julian's hand under her elbow was warm and sure, like she had imagined his lips would be after that fateful evening at The Queen's Arms. She deemed it a horrid weakness of character, but ever since Julian had nearly kissed her, Lily had sincerely regretted Pleshy's interruption. Quite a lowering admission to make, because she could not imagine Julian respecting her at all once she had allowed his flirtatious trifling to be consummated with a kiss and embrace. For that was all it was, wasn't it—flirtatious trifling? But if he could trifle with her, why did she still think of him as the perfect man?

The library door closed behind them. A fire had been lit in the grate, as if the servants had anticipated their master's desire to sit there that evening. The heavy, solid furnishings gleamed with bees wax, and the smell of old leather and conservatory flowers wafted on the air. A vase of yellow cabbage roses stood on a table by a large, plush chair near the fireplace. Prints of Winslow ancestors co-mingled with more landscapes on the forest green walls. The room exactly suited Julian—elegant, understated, masculine and warm.

Her brief perusal of the library ended when she felt Julian looking at her. Their eyes met, that current of awareness pulsating between them as before. He took her hand and led her to a sofa near the fire. She sat down, their eyes never breaking connection during the entire removal to the couch. He did not let go her hand, and she made no attempt to snatch it away. She was mesmerized by the golden magnificence of The Lion's eyes. And if this moment was all she was destined to have in such close and tantalizing proximity to Julian, she would take it gladly.

"Lily...I may call you Lily, mightn't I? We've been through quite a lot together." His voice was low and gentle, caressing.

Lily nodded her head, barely able to breathe, much less speak. He was stroking the palm of her hand with the firm pad of his thumb.

"You are wondering what I have to say to you which cannot be said in front of my sister?"

Again Lily nodded.

He glanced down at her small hand, encased as it was in his much larger one. "You have been a sore trial to me, Lily," he began, and Lily felt a stab of pain in her chest. Oh, dear, was he going to tell her what a nuisance she'd been and, from some chivalrous notion of honour and kindness, lecture her again about her foolhardy and meddlesome propensities?

"I'm sorry I've caused you any trouble, my lord. I never meant to," she mumbled, her heart breaking.

He surprised her by emitting a low chuckle. "Never say so! I don't believe you can be sorry about Sebastian, or Belle, or Nort, whatever you might say! And neither can I!"

She was much puzzled, and searched his face for some clue as to his meaning. She saw tenderness writ in every feature, and his eyes glowed with strong emotion. What emotion? she wondered.

"The only thing I regret, Lily, is that I didn't meet you sooner, that I wasn't there to snatch you the moment you emerged from the schoolroom!"

Lily's throat constricted with feeling. Her fingers wrapped about Julian's thumb. "What are you saying, my lord? Please don't trifle with me! You see, there's no need for flummery! And you mustn't think that because I wanted you to kiss me... No, I didn't mean that! That is, just because I might have *let* you kiss me if Pleshy hadn't interrupted us when he did, does *not* mean that I—''

Julian tugged his thumb out of Lily's agitated grip, as that appendage was turning rather blue, and firmly clasped her shoulders with both hands. He looked into her astonished brown eyes and said, "How many times do I have to tell you, my dear girl, that my compliments to you are quite sincere—not flummery in the least! And when I nearly kissed you, I had not been indulging the whims of a libertine, rather I was compelled to kiss you for reasons entirely spontaneous and genuine! It seems I've fallen in love with you, my *dear* troublesome little baggage! And I have no intention of allowing you to go one way in the world and myself in the other direction! Who will extricate you from the scrapes you will tumble into day after day? On whose estate will you farm out sundry animals and criminals and unhappy chits on their way to loveless marriages? Who, my dearest, *who?*''

Lily's eyes were filled with happy tears. She blinked through the salty blur and smiled at Julian. "But you said that philanthropy was fatiguing and inconvenient, my lord! You said—''

Julian sobered. "I said a great many selfish, foolish things, Lily, for all of which I hope you may forgive me. I am a changed man, or maybe something like the man I used to be. I still have a long way to go in forming my character, and I hope you will help me!

All I know is that I want to spend the rest of my life with you, no matter how fatiguing it may prove to be. With my hard-headed realism and your charitable heart, we might contrive to do very well together.''

"Oh, Julian!" exclaimed Lily, cupping his face in her hands and smiling brightly up at him. "You're such a *good* man, and I do love you so!"

"No more than I love you!" he answered gruffly, then pulled her against him for that long-awaited kiss, making quite sure that the wait was well worth it. Several moments later, with Lily's hair even more tumbled than before, and even Julian's hair gone a bit awry from Lily's shameless running of her fingers through the long, golden locks, she wedged her hands between them and pushed Julian gently away.

Her mind fogged with euphoria and a green girl's first passion, Lily nonetheless faintly enquired, "What about Peter, Julian? I know he doesn't truly love me, but he thinks he does. Do we dare tell him now? I don't wish him to fall into the megrims and make himself sick. I know it's silly, but I think he might take it rather hard!"

Julian straightened up and endeavoured to control his breathing. Lily saw the up-and-down motion of his chest and blushed at the idea that she could actually be the cause of such delightsome discomposure. "Peter's not a child any longer, Lily, and we're going to tell him tonight! Even if we postponed the announcement, judging by the effect you have on me I don't think I would be able to disguise my feelings for you for more than a few minutes, anyway! Then he would be angry that we hadn't told him in the first place!''

Lily's forehead wrinkled in thought. ''I suppose you're right, but—''

There was a knock on the door. They looked at each other, Julian's tawny brows lifting enquiringly. Then they hastily tried to restore themselves to a semblance of order, straightening a puffed sleeve here, a neckcloth there, et cetera. They scooted apart about twelve inches. Finally Julian called out in a tolerably normal voice, ''Come!''

Winny stepped into the room, grinning knowingly as she surveyed their flushed and dishevelled appearances. She approached with a kind of swagger, stationed herself directly in front of the sofa, and rubbed her hands together in the manner of a miser surveying his cache of coins. ''I love weddings,'' she informed them irrepressibly. ''When will yours be?''

Julian laughed and reached his arm behind Lily to pull her close to him. ''That has not been discussed as yet, but you can be sure it will be soon.''

Winny bent over and gave Lily a hug. ''Welcome, little sister! I'm eternally grateful to you for saving this dear man from his own bitterness! Indeed, you *are* a guardian angel! First you save Peter, then you save Julian!''

''We were just speaking of Peter,'' said Lily, her smile faltering. ''He has been used to thinking of me in a certain way over the past weeks. We're a little concerned that when we tell him about us, he'll—''

Winny straightened and looked rather smug, which was not the attitude Lily had expected. "Peter already knows, so neither of you need fret about *that!*"

"But Winifred," Julian exclaimed, much surprised, "how did he react? And who's with him, for heaven's sake?"

"In answer to your first question, he took it just as you thought he might. He woke up from his nap right after you left, when I had just barely laid my hand on his brow to check for a fever. He was too excited at being home to sleep deeply, I suspect. When he enquired where you'd gone, I was inspired to tell him the whole truth immediately. There is never anything to be gained by procrastination, you know! Besides, judging by the way the two of you have been looking at each other just since you arrived tonight, I rather suspected that Peter had an inkling of what was afoot, anyway. And, yes, he admitted that he'd suspected a growing attachment between the two of you, but tried to ignore what his eyes and ears clearly told him."

"Is he blue-deviled, then?" Julian prompted her.

"He was at first, but I scolded him about it, telling him that sometimes people are destined to be together in this life. I've always believed that, you know. I truly believe that Edward and I made a pact before we came to this earth, to share our lives here. I told him that you and Lily were perfect for each other, and that he— Peter, you know—had probably been the divinely directed means of bringing you together!"

"And that bag of moonshine resigned him to his loss?" Julian remarked with dry good humour.

"Julian, I thought you had changed!" complained Winny, laughing.

"Not *that* much!" Julian said, winking at his sister.

"Well, you're quite right, of course. My theory of predestination did not exactly soothe his wounded heart, but then the Cavendish twins arrived for dinner and I—"

"The Cavendish twins!" exclaimed Lily, much diverted. "How did you *think* to do such a thing, Winny? Why, it is the perfect antidote for Peter's megrims!"

Winny pursed her lips in a pondering pose. "Once again, I can only suppose that I was inspired to send word to them after Pleshy arrived, letting them know that Peter was expected this evening. They have enquired about him regularly, you know. On an impulse, I also invited them to dinner. I knew Peter would be fatigued, but he has always been so close to Lizzy and Lucinda—"

"Don't excuse yourself, Winny," said Julian. "There's no need. You couldn't have hit on a better welcome for Peter. He may be tired, but the company of good friends will do him a world of good."

"If he finds them as jolly and pretty as he did before, maybe he'll eventually offer for one of them," suggested Lily. "The only thing is, he'll have to choose between the two, and perhaps he'll never be able to do so!''

Once again Winny looked highly self-satisfied. ''That won't be a problem. You see, Lizzy's been engaged these six weeks! She long ago relegated her feelings for Peter to a sisterly affection, but Lucinda still pines for him, poor dear!'' Winny's face brightened. ''But now he has only to make up his mind about *one* Cavendish twin, and seeing them together tonight makes me rather hopeful! Come, you two, judge for yourself! Come and look at them!'' Then Winny exited the room, apparently unable to stay long away from her son and the young lady she hoped soon to call daughter.

Lily allowed herself to be pulled to her feet by Julian, but declined the idea of presenting herself in the drawing-room in such a travel-worn state, her disarray compounded by the caressive pawings of her dear Lion. She would discover where her room was and freshen up first, if he didn't mind.

Julian tucked a stray wisp of chestnut brown hair behind Lily's ear, his loving gaze travelling over the delicate features of her face as if to memorize them exactly. ''I'll let you out of my sight now, my dear little vicarage child. But do not loiter, or I shall have to come fetch you!''

Lily stroked Julian's jacket lapel and looked coy. ''Goodness, was that a threat? Do you imagine I'm afraid of you, my lord? If you must know, my dear husband-to-be, while I admittedly tremble in fright at the appearance of a wee rodent, I shan't be put into a quake by the roaring of my very *own* pet lion!''

Julian growled and pulled her roughly against him, and Lily fearlessly returned his embrace.

EPILOGUE

PEEKING THROUGH the draperies at Ashton House ten years after the marriage of Julian Winslow, Lord Ashton, to Miss Lilith Clarke, lately of Whitfield in the County of Kent, one might observe any number of interesting happenstances.

For example, on Christmas Day, 1825, Peter and Lucinda came to show off their infant sons, a set of twins. The twins were the most recent additions to their hopeful family of four. Peter fully and quickly recovered from his illness, *and* his disappointed love, with the help of the timely blossoming of Miss Lucinda Cavendish, who, at the advanced age of three-and-twenty, became the most beautiful woman of Peter's acquaintance. It did not hurt, either, that she was as jolly as she had ever been as a girl and was still not averse to horseplay.

Much to Julian's pleased astonishment, Pleshy and Janet married, too. Pleshy stepped down from his position as valet to tackle the challenge of farming, and soon discovered that he was as talented in this area as he had been in the area of rigging out Lord Ashton in the first stare of fashion. They prospered despite the speedy introduction of five little Pleshys into the world and their mother's preference for romping and turning cartwheels with the little dears over other more domestic duties. Pleshy cherished Janet's love of life and, with steadfast devotion, helped her forget all about that early part of her life which had not been so gay.

At six-and-twenty, comely Belle still had not married, but she didn't seem to mind in the least. She proved to be much more than "deedy" about the house. In fact, she was so very good at everything she did that she soon was promoted to a sort of under-housekeeper, ready to step into Mrs. Strand's shoes when that lady decided to retire and live with her widowed sister in Harrogate. Not that Belle was anxious to usurp Mrs. Strand's position, for she loved the older woman dearly and had begun to look upon her as a sort of foster mother. The feeling was entirely mutual and Mrs. Strand often thanked his lordship for bringing dear little Belle to Ashton House.

Norton Bickford came to collect his deed and his gun, his family of four children and a surprisingly diminutive wife in tow. Pleshy and Norton became neighbours and friends and often discussed crop philosophy over a tankard of ale. Due to their mutual interest in modern farming and the sharing of tried-and-true methods of cultivation, they both enjoyed a comfortable living.

A rumour had once been heard that Nort was a reformed highwayman, but it was quickly put to bed.

No one as gentle and mild-mannered as "Ol' Nort" could ever have held anyone at gunpoint, thereby flirting stupidly with the looped end of a rope. When their fifth child was born—another son—Norton asked Lord Ashton's permission to christen him Julian. Urged by Lily to disregard his natural, humble aversion to such a tribute, Julian finally graciously accepted. Ironically, "Jule," as he was nicknamed, turned out to be the naughtiest of their entire brood.

Sebastian was Peter's faithful companion till he left his very comfortable mortal existence for cat heaven. When Peter stayed in London, he even went so far as to sport Sebastian about Town in his curricle, Sebastian reposed in all his regal furriness just next to him on the seat. This started a new fashion, and carriage cats became all the rage, which happenstance of Sebastian's sojourn on Earth became a fitting eulogy for so devoted a pet. However, Sebastian was so obliging as to leave behind several look-alike offspring, so that Peter might always have a yellow cat as companion for as long as he chose to keep one. And he *did* choose to keep a yellow cat at his side till the end of his days.

As for Julian and Lily, life was as adventuresome as Julian predicted at the start. Their house quickly filled up with cats, serving effectively both as rodent deterrents and four-legged hot bricks. But the army-like number of children they'd mutually agreed to bring into the world was not to be. Lily lost one child before she delivered a son, named Richard Thomas after Julian's two brothers. However, after Richy's robust entry into life, there were no other conceptions.

Satisfied with his hearty little heir, and his beloved wife's continued good health despite her inability to conceive another child, Julian suggested that they adopt a brother or a sister for Richy. Lily, never behindhand in pursuing an idea which greatly appealed to her, quickly swelled the number of children at Ashton House to five. Richy acquired two sisters and two brothers, all of differing ages, looks and backgrounds, from a foundling home in Holybourne, which was the nearest town. There would have been more, but Julian knew that if the line was not drawn somewhere, his philanthropic little wife would turn the house into an orphanage, with five children in each room!

Sundry unfortunates continually came in the way of the Winslow family over the years, and the poor wretches were always fed and clothed and sent on their way with references for employment or at least some good, sound advice and a few golden coins. However, Julian was occasionally called upon to thwart the unscrupulous designs of practised scapegraces intent on taking advantage of the notoriously generous Lady Ashton. Always alert to the possibility of such abuse, Julian earned a reputation for being as swift to serve retribution to those who deserved it as he was to extend a helping hand. He was a good man, there could be no doubt about that. But he was cunning, too, not easily fooled or trifled with.

As for the Clarke family, the vicar and his wife and progeny frequently visited Ashton House, bringing with them all the noise and disorder of Whitfield Vicarage to mingle with the noise and disorder of Ashton House—which, indeed, had become just such another beatific bedlam.

As for the ton, they missed Julian's wit and handsome looks, but enjoyed for some time the fascinating story of his return to rural hermitage, and of the little vicarage mouse who had fearlessly pulled the thorn of bitterness from The Lion's paw.

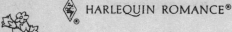

HARLEQUIN ROMANCE®

**Harlequin Romance
has love in
store for you!**

Don't miss next
month's title in

THE BRIDAL COLLECTION

A WHOLESALE ARRANGEMENT
by Day Leclaire

THE BRIDE *needed* the Groom.
THE GROOM *wanted* the Bride.
BUT THE WEDDING was *more* than
a convenient solution!

Available this month in
The Bridal Collection
Only Make-Believe
by Bethany Campbell
Harlequin Romance #3230

Available wherever Harlequin books are sold.

WED-8

HE CROSSED TIME FOR HER

Captain Richard Colter rode the high seas, brandished a sword and pillaged treasure ships. A swashbuckling privateer, he was a man with voracious appetites and a lust for living. And in the eighteenth century, any woman swooned at his feet for the favor of his wild passion. History had it that Captain Richard Colter went down with his ship, the *Black Cutter,* in a dazzling sea battle off the Florida coast in 1792.

Then what was he doing washed ashore on a Key West beach in 1992—alive?

MARGARET ST. GEORGE brings you an extraspecial love story this month, about an extraordinary man who would do anything for the woman he loved:

#462 THE PIRATE AND HIS LADY
by Margaret St. George

When love is meant to be, nothing can stand in its way...not even time.

Don't miss American Romance
#462 THE PIRATE AND HIS LADY.
It's a love story you'll never forget.

HARLEQUIN ROMANCE®

After her father's heart attack, Stephanie Bloomfield comes home to Orchard Valley, Oregon, to be with him and with her sisters.

Orchard Valley

Steffie learns that many things have changed in her absence—but not her feelings for journalist Charles Tomaselli. He was the reason she left Orchard Valley. Now, three years later, will he give her a reason to stay?

"The Orchard Valley trilogy features three delightful, spirited sisters and a trio of equally fascinating men. The stories are rich with the romance, warmth of heart and humor readers expect, and invariably receive, from Debbie Macomber."
—Linda Lael Miller

Don't miss the Orchard Valley trilogy by Debbie Macomber:

VALERIE   Harlequin Romance #3232 (November 1992)
STEPHANIE   Harlequin Romance #3239 (December 1992)
NORAH   Harlequin Romance #3244 (January 1993)

Look for the special cover flash on each book!

Available wherever Harlequin books are sold.   ORC-2

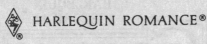

HARLEQUIN ROMANCE®

Some people have the spirit
of Christmas all year round...

People like Blake Connors
and Karin Palmer.

Meet them—and love them!—in
Eva Rutland's
ALWAYS CHRISTMAS.

· HARLEQUIN ·
HISTORICAL

CHRISTMAS

· STORIES · 1992 ·

Capture the magic and romance of Christmas in the 1800s
with HARLEQUIN HISTORICAL CHRISTMAS STORIES
1992—a collection of three stories by celebrated
historical authors. The perfect Christmas gift!

Don't miss these heartwarming stories, available in
November wherever Harlequin books are sold:

MISS MONTRACHET REQUESTS by Maura Seger
CHRISTMAS BOUNTY by Erin Yorke
A PROMISE KEPT by Bronwyn Williams

Plus, this Christmas you can also receive a FREE
keepsake Christmas ornament. Watch for details in all
November and December Harlequin books.

DISCOVER THE ROMANCE AND MAGIC OF THE
HOLIDAY SEASON WITH HARLEQUIN HISTORICAL
CHRISTMAS STORIES!